Revenge is a Dish Best Served with Eggnog

A COZY PARANORMAL MYSTERY

ADA RAYNE

Book Cover & Illustrations by Cosmic Cupcake

1st edition December 2023

Chapter One

Destiny let out an exasperated sigh as she taped up the final gift basket. It was the week before Christmas and the little gift shop that belonged to her parents was bursting with holiday cheer. Garlands of evergreen and twinkling lights adorned every shelf, while festive tunes played over the speakers. But Destiny was in no mood to celebrate.

"I swear, if I have to look at another speck of glitter, I'm going to scream," she muttered under her breath.

It was the same every year. Her parents went overboard with the holiday kitsch, turning their little gift shop into a winter wonderland explosion. Which meant Destiny got roped into creating all kinds of wacky gift baskets and arrangements. Like this one — filled with wooden figurines of animals and holiday-scented candles, then doused in enough glitter to supply an army of Abba impersonators.

Destiny wrinkled her nose as she sprinkled a final snowfall of shiny flecks over the cellophane wrap. Why did everything cute have to be ruined by being dipped in glitter? She imagined it getting everywhere - coating the floors and shelves, sticking to her hair and clothes. Just thinking about it made her eye twitch.

At least this was the last monstrosity on her list. She affixed a sticker saying "Have Yourself a Twinkly Little Christmas!" and suppressed a gag. With more force than necessary, she plopped the basket on the shelf amidst twenty others just like it.

"All done!" she announced to no one in particular. The faster they sold this glitter bomb, the better.

Destiny glanced over at the life-sized nutcracker soldiers that flanked the shop's front door. Their painted smiles and rosy cheeks mocked her grumpy mood.

"Oh be quiet," she told them with a scowl. "You wouldn't look so jolly if you had to decorate this glitter factory every year."

Just then, the front door opened abruptly and a gust of wind blew glitter everywhere. The nutcrackers said nothing, but Destiny could swear their grins grew wider. She rolled her eyes and attempted to blow a strand of her hair out of her eye.

She glanced up to say hello, but the man had halted in the middle of the store, studying her. What was he thinking? Probably she wasn't fast enough with her greeting. “Hello and happy holidays. How may I help you?”

The man approached the counter with an easy smile. "Excuse me, I was wondering if you could point me towards the Christmas Hills Resort? I just got into town but I'm afraid I've gotten a bit turned around."

Destiny felt an instinctive flutter of interest as she met his warm hazel eyes, though she quickly tempered it. She had no intention of being swayed by a charming newcomer, no matter how appealing.

"It's just a few miles up the main road, you can't miss it," she replied briskly. She noticed him subtly studying her in return before he nodded.

“Thanks. I hate to admit I’m lost. But I appreciate your directions. I thought my phone would get me there, but I lost service, then it went dead. When I restarted and plugged in the address, it pointed me here. I'm Carson, by the way," he added with a grin, holding out his hand.

Destiny shook it, trying not to focus too much on the pleasant tingle of his grip. "Destiny. "

The door blew open again, and a man rushed in glancing at his watch with a furrowed brow, and brought all the trappings of winter in with him; the whistling wind, his heavy breath, and cold air.

“Goodness, it’s mighty cold out there.”

“Yes. Still snowing too,” Carson said.

“May I help you?” she asked.

The older gentleman slapped his gloved hands together. “Oh, I’m Blake. I’m here for the photo.”

“Oh, yes.” She thought she knew everyone in town, but it had changed so much over the years she’d been gone. “It’s all ready for you.”

Blake's eyes darted around the cozy space filled with holiday knick-knacks until they landed on a distinctive package sitting on the counter. He thundered over and picked up the package. “It looks beautiful. Thank you so much. Would you tell your parents how much I appreciate what they’ve done?”

"Absolutely. They said you'd received and approved the final piece by email and it was okay to gift wrap it. Are you sure you don't want to see it in person?"

"No, no. I'm sure it's perfect."

"You've settled everything with them, so you're all set."

"Thanks a bunch! Well, I've got a flight to catch. Really appreciate you getting this done, Destiny."

"No problem at all," Destiny replied warmly as Blake toddled out of the store without so much as a backward glance. She then turned back to Carson, who was watching the interaction with interest.

She whooshed out a breath. "Why would anyone think that's a good idea?"

"I'm sorry?"

"Oh, uh." She flicked a piece of hair from her face, mostly imaginary. "That gift. A photo of a ring. Black and white. Not even a real ring." She shrugged. "I don't understand the concept." She had no idea why she'd just told him that.

"Maybe they are renewing their vows," he said, then continued, "or celebrating an anniversary. Maybe it's a photo of her actual ring, and instead of getting her a new one, he wanted to gift her the first one he ever slipped on her finger."

Heat flushed her face. "Okay, I guess I didn't think of it like that."

"Do you still have it?"

"Have what?"

"The photo. I heard you tell him you sent him an email of the final piece, so I thought you'd have a copy."

“Oh, the photo. Yes, we keep the digital versions just in case there’s a problem with the order. Let me pull it up on the computer.”

Carson peered over the counter, catching a glimpse of the ring's sparkle. “Wow,” he said. “Yes, this is great. A masterpiece, really. And it’s definitely a wedding anniversary.”

Destiny glanced up, meeting his earnest gaze. "You think so?"

"Absolutely," Carson said. "Jewelry gifts hold symbolic weight - the metal and stones lasting through lifetimes, passed down to honor those we cherish. That framed ring looks like it's from a different era, an heirloom ring like that carries a world of meaning."

He gently admired the image on the computer. "And the fact it's showcased like this? That suggests proudly displaying that significance for all to see."

Destiny nodded, intrigued by Carson's sentimental perspective. "You're quite the romantic, I hadn't thought of it like that. Now I'm sold on this idea." She found herself unexpectedly charmed.

Carson laughed self-consciously. "Guilty as charged. Using words and images to imbue meaning is my specialty." He smiled ruefully. "My version of romance, anyway."

Destiny smiled back, feeling intrigue as well as an undeniable connection. For a moment, she let her guard down, warmed by Carson's charming sensitivity.

Just then, a cat with a plush white tail swishing behind her sauntered onto the counter seemingly out of nowhere. Her fur was predominantly snowy white, accented by soft grey tabby stripes that wrapped around her legs and swirled artfully along her back and face. Her eyes, one blue and one green, took in the shop with curiosity, and her plush grey nose twitched as she sniffed the holiday aroma in the air.

She swished her tail in the glitter, then rubbed and snuggled up to Destiny.

“Why do you always do this, Velvet?”

“A beautiful cat,” he said, attempting to pet Velvet yet avoid glitter madness.

“Isn't she? And her eyes are peculiar.”

He smiled. He once heard a myth that cats with different colored eyes had special abilities, although he wasn’t about to ask the cat’s owner about that.

Destiny busied herself tidying the gift wrap counter, avoiding the handsome stranger's gaze, which seemed to be stirring an unwanted flutter in her stomach.

"So you grew up here in Christmas Hills?" he asked.

Destiny nodded, focusing on the glitter-sweeping. "Born and raised. But I moved away for a long time. Just came back a short while ago."

She chanced a glance at the man, catching his look of interest. His tousled brown hair and athletic build hinted at a lively spirit beneath the tailored business casual attire.

"So what brings you to Christmas Hills all by your lonesome for the holidays?" she asked, brushing a stray lock of mocha hair from her eyes.

Carson chuckled, raking a hand through his sandy brown hair. "Actually, I'm here on a work-mandated holiday. My boss seems to think my creativity has flatlined, and unless I can get my Christmas spirit back, I'll be looking for a new job come January."

"A work-mandated holiday?" Destiny raised an eyebrow. "What on earth does that mean?"

"Well, I'm in advertising," Carson explained, leaning against the counter. "And according to my superiors, my holiday ad concepts have been drier than the Sahara desert. So they've banished me here to Christmas Hills for a couple of weeks to soak up the holiday atmosphere. Long story short, I'm here to rekindle my Christmas joy, save my job, and hopefully get them to stop calling me by that annoying nickname."

"What nickname?"

"Satan is an anagram of Santa and they like to call me that since I'm so blah-humbug about the holidays." Carson rolled his eyes and shrugged.

Destiny pressed her lips together, stifling a laugh.

“What about you?” he asked, trying to continue their earlier conversation.

“What about me what?”

"What made you decide to come back after being away so long?" Carson asked.

Destiny hesitated. She wasn't keen on revealing too much about herself to anyone, least of all a near-total stranger, but something about him made her more talkative than normal. "Denver was my last stop. Tried to make a name for myself as a chef." Destiny fiddled with the glitter shakers. "Things didn't work out how I planned. So here I am, back home helping my parents during the holidays."

She forced brightness into her tone. This stranger didn't need to know about the details of her broken dreams. The less said about why she had fled back to the shelter of Christmas Hills, the better.

Carson nodded, though his gaze suggested he suspected there was more to her story. Thankfully, he didn't pry. "Well, Christmas Hills is lucky to have you back, even if just for a little while," he said with a crooked smile.

Destiny felt her cheeks grow warm and busied herself straightening a display of gift bags.

"You know," sensing her discomfort, Carson changed the subject swiftly. "I've had this charging for hours now. It came on and pointed me here and then went off again. Any chance you carry cell phone chargers here?"

"You can borrow mine," she dug into her purse and pulled out a charger.

"That's great!" He said came around the other side of the counter where she plugged the charger into the wall and handed her his phone.

"It doesn't show it's charging, but probably takes a few minutes." She set the phone on the counter.

"While we wait, can you help me find my joy of Christmas?" he asked. When her eyes narrowed, he hurried along. "I mean, by pointing me in the right direction."

She gave a half shrug. "I could circle a few things on the map, sure. You've come to the right place if you need Christmas spirit intervention. The Christmas Hills Resort up on Peak View Road is world-famous for its holiday magic. My friend Kari is the head chef up there. Every year they go all out - carolers, carriage rides, the biggest tree you've ever seen, not to mention the tree-lighting ceremony. People travel from all over just to soak it up. Honestly, I've always found the whole production a bit overwhelming."

“You don’t love the holiday season like the rest of this town does?” he asked, enamored by her.

"Well, let's just say the holidays and I aren't on great terms these days," she concluded lightly. "But if anything can restore your Christmas mojo, the Christmas Hills Resort is your best bet."

Carson's eyes lit up with a sudden spark of inspiration as he listened to Destiny.

"You know what? I have an idea," he said, leaning forward eagerly. "Since neither of us is feeling the Christmas spirit these days, why don't we make a pact to help each other out? We can be accountability partners and do festive stuff together to get ourselves back in the holiday mood."

Destiny raised an eyebrow skeptically. "What, like your own personal Christmas elves?"

Carson laughed. "Something like that! I'm stuck in this winter wonderland for two weeks minimum. And you clearly know the place inside out. So why not join forces? With your insider expertise of Christmas Hills and my unjaded outsider perspective, we're bound to rub off on each other."

An intriguing proposal, though she wasn't about to let her guard down, no matter how appealing the company was. "I’m the last person anyone should look for to find any Christmas joy." She handed Carson his phone back, still dead. "And it looks like my charger isn't working for your phone."

Carson's face fell slightly at Destiny's dismissive response. Clearly, she was even more resistant to the holiday spirit than he was. But he wasn't ready to give up on her just yet.

First things first though - he needed to get his phone working again. Carson picked it up from the table and frowned.

"Well shoot," he muttered. "Is there another store nearby that might have a good selection of wireless chargers? Maybe it's my plug that's on the fritz."

Destiny nodded towards the shop window. "Pat's General Store just down the street is your best bet. Pat's got a little bit of everything - I'm sure he'll have something that can help."

"Great, thanks," Carson said, tucking his useless phone into his pocket. "I'll head over there right now and see what I can find."

He moved towards the exit but paused with his hand on the door. Turning back to Destiny, he gave her a hopeful smile.

"What time are you open till?"

Destiny looked at the cuckoo clock on the wall. "I'll be here for another hour or so. By the way - you might want a heavier jacket for strolling about. The climate in the mountains can become extremely cold quickly, and there are lots of Christmas activities at the resort both indoors and outdoors."

Carson looked touched by her concern. "Thanks. See you later."

With a wink, Carson headed out the door, bells jingling merrily in his wake. Destiny watched him go, a smile playing about her lips. This holiday season might just shape up to be interesting after all.

Chapter Two

Destiny gazed after the handsome stranger as he exited the gift shop. She felt an undeniable spark of attraction towards the charming Carson, yet hesitated to act on it. After all, Christmas and romance had never boded well for her.

As if on cue, Velvet sauntered in, purring a greeting. Destiny's fluffy white cat with stripes of gray trotted over to rub against her ankle, meowing for attention. Despite being nearly seven years old, Velvet's oversized eyes and ears lent her a perpetual kittenish air.

"Well hello again, cutie pie," Destiny cooed as she scooped up the affectionate feline. "What do you think of that nice man I was just talking to?"

Velvet nuzzled under her chin, purring contentedly.

Destiny sighed, giving the cat a squeeze. "You're right, I shouldn't get ahead of myself."

Yes, Destiny mused as she cuddled Velvet's soft fur, she had ample reason to be cautious. Though a part of her, an optimistic part she had thought long buried, whispered that maybe, just maybe, this Christmas could be different.

CARSON DECIDED the walk would do him some good, and exhaled a frosty breath as he wandered down the snow-lined street. But not even a block later, he realized the cold affected him a lot more than he expected.

Texas wind could be brutal, but this cold squeezed into his bones and made everything tense. The shop girl was right about the jacket. He could have turned around and got into his car, but he needed to clear his head. His meeting with Destiny had disconcerted him. The mixture of light brown and gold in her irises reminded him of gemstones like citrine and Baltic amber. He cursed his phone. All the ideas flowing through his mind right now, and he didn't have a way to jot them down. He should always carry a small paper notepad with him.

He jammed his hands into his coat pockets, replaying their banter. Her gemstone eyes glinted with intelligence, yet wariness too. The way she deftly deflected his inquiries while still hinting at shadows beneath the surface. Carson found her combination of sweetness and steel appeal irresistible.

THE BRISK WALK did him well. He relaxed his shoulders despite the cold and admired the charming storefronts adorned with glittering lights and festive wreaths. The faint sound of jingle bells filled the crisp mountain air as he approached Pat's General Store. As he stepped inside, the rich scents of cinnamon and pine washed over him, mingling with the aroma of freshly baked cookies. An animatronic Santa greeted him at the door.

"Ho ho ho! Merry Christmas. Help you find anything?" Carson jumped at the deep, jovial voice, disoriented at how human it sounded. Too human to have come from the animatronic Santa. He looked around and saw that behind the counter stood a robust, bearded man dressed in a full Santa Claus ensemble, complete with black boots and a crimson cap.

Carson glanced at the fake Santa near the door, then the real man behind the counter, who was now finger-brushing his beard.

“Don’t worry. I grow it out this time every year, and the speckles of gray are given a delicate touch of white with my wife’s hair dye. We go all out every Christmas. The kids love it, and they’re convinced Santa’s secret shop is behind my store,” he explained in a boomy, jolly voice, sensing his customer’s trepidation.

Carson chuckled, immediately put at ease by the shopkeeper's theatrical spirit. "Well if it isn't Kris Kringle himself," he quipped, sauntering up to the counter.

"Now what can Santa get for you today?"

“Need a phone charger and a coat.”

“Got plenty of those.” He toddled from behind his counter and patted his belly. “This isn’t fake, unfortunately.”

Carson laughed. “You look great.”

“Here you are.” The man stopped at a row of charging plugs and phone accessories. “We get a lot of travelers, especially this time of year. So I try to stock as many different ones as I can. Any particular type you're looking for?"

Carson explained the odd behavior of his phone and that it had not been successfully charging. "I think the USB plug might be broken. Maybe I should try a wireless charger."

The man's eyes crinkled at him. "Yeah. We get a lot of that around here too."

"What do you mean?"

"Christmas magic. Newbies come into town, lodge in the resort and phones don't work for a few days." He picked up a charger. "Don't worry. It'll come back on. It's just magic's way of telling you to enjoy what's around you, instead of what's on your phone. Here, let's give this one a try."

He gestured to a wireless charger on the counter. "Best give it some juice before heading up, just in case."

Carson obliged, setting his phone on the pad.

"I'll show you where the coats are if you come this way," the burly man nodded and trekked through the store, waving Carson over. "Name's Pat, by the way."

"Carson."

"Most people call me Santa this time of year."

Cason laughed. "Most people call me Satan this time of year."

Pat stopped and turned, eyes narrowing. "Why's that?"

"Well. I tend to overwork this time of year. And I get a little cranky. My coworkers don't understand and tend to get aggravated with me when I ask them to stay a little past the hour. Their families at home don't like me either."

Pat nodded, mouth pursing. "Mmm hmm."

"That's why I'm here. Because I'm short on holiday spirit and need to find my Christmas joy."

They stopped at a slew of coats, and Carson's stomach dropped. He's not about to dress up looking like a lumberjack.

"Wow. How am I supposed to choose?"

Pat picked a coat from the rack and removed it from its hanger. A soft gray with a touch of blue. "Why don't you try this one?"

Carson removed his jacket and tried on the coat. Despite the style, it's instant gratification. He stuffed his hands into the pockets. The coat moved with him, offering him warmth without being too bulky.

"This is perfect." He pulled it off and handed it back to Pat, surprising himself.

Pat waved him off. "If that's the one you want, might as well keep it on. Anything else I can help you with?"

"This covers it for now."

Carson held both jackets in his hands—the new one and his older one. The room was warm enough, so he didn't need anything right now.

Pat paused midway. "I think there's something else you'll need. We haven't had a reason to stock it until last year, and um, we don't give it out to everyone. But, I like you."

Carson was more confused than ever, and his face didn't hide the fact. Pat smiled and handed him a postcard-sized, flat and oval-shaped metal object with tiny holes and a big hole and other impressions on it.

"When things start to get weird, you might need to communicate with what perturbs you. It's better than not even being able to communicate with it"

Carson blinked. He wasn't the most adept at social cues, but he knew the message Pat was trying to pass. Small towns had their own intrigue and belief, and they got messy at times, better to just go with it. He put the object in his wallet, sure to keep it safe.

They walked back to the counter, where Pat rang up his purchases and Carson checked his phone again. To his dismay, the screen remained a smooth black mirror with no sign of life.

"Well now, seems the resort wants your full attention," Pat mused. "Don't worry, I'm sure your phone will power on eventually."

He handed over the package with the charger. Carson took it and pulled on his new coat.

"I'm starting to think maybe you are actually Santa Claus," Carson said.

Pat chuckled. "Why's that?"

"The perfect coat. The perfect charger. And that, nice piece of metal souvenir. Got everything I needed in record time."

Pat's smile sparkled across his entire face, almost making Carson a believer. He pointed to a box at the door.

"You can keep your other jacket if you want. But we also have a donation drop box right there where we take new and used coats."

"Oh, sure, absolutely. And why don't you add another new one to that box as well?" He pulled out some cash from his wallet to cover the expense of a new jacket like the one he just bought.

Pat nodded and took the cash. “Thank you. I appreciate that, and I know others will too.”

They shook hands. “Thank you, Santa Pat. Until next time.”

CARSON STEPPED BACK into the warmth of the gift shop, shaking snowflakes from his hair. Destiny looked up from arranging a display of handmade ornaments and felt a flutter in her chest at the sight of his crooked smile.

"Well don't you look sharp," she said, nodding at the charcoal peacoat he wore. "New coat?"

Carson glanced down, smoothing a hand over the wool. "Just picked it up from Santa Pat. You know what they say about new coats though..." He trailed off with a dramatic sigh.

Destiny tilted her head. "What's that?"

"The pockets are always too empty." Carson flashed a roguish wink.

With a laugh, Destiny turned and printed out a copy of the framed ring photo. She held it out to Carson. "Maybe this will bring you some luck."

He accepted the picture, glancing at it with a soft smile before tucking it into his pocket. "Thanks, I'll carry it as a good luck charm during my stay here."

"DID Santa Pat help you find a charger for your phone too?"

Carson sighed and shook his head.

"No luck huh?" Destiny asked, looking up from arranging a display.

"Nope, this thing is dead as a doornail," Carson grumbled. He slipped the phone back into his pocket. "Say, would you want to grab dinner later? I was hoping to check out that tree-lighting ceremony at the resort tonight too. Maybe you could show me the way since my GPS is out of commission?"

Destiny's eyes widened briefly before her expression shifted to a coy smile. "Oh, um, I would but..." She trailed off, biting her lip as she pretended to contemplate a response. "I promised my grandma I would... help her bake cookies for the annual cookie exchange."

"Maybe she could spare you for one evening?" Carson said. He leaned against the counter, amusement glinting in his eyes.

“I think I’m good to not go,” she said.

“But you shouldn’t miss it,” he started, “Besides, two grinches would make the ceremony a lot easier to deal with.”

It probably would do her some good to get out and go. To see what all the fuss was about. Besides, hadn’t she promised herself to find a bit of joy this season? At least convince her parents she wasn’t a real Grinch.

“But then, I would be driving back home in the dark,” she said.

Not that it mattered. She had great night vision, and she’d taken much more treacherous roads before. Not to mention she knows that mountain like the back of her hand and the resort was literally a ten-minute drive from her home.

"I could drive you back down the mountain," he said without hesitation.

"That's kind of you, but..." Destiny tapped her chin pensively before snapping her fingers. "I'm volunteering at the animal shelter later and really can't miss my shift."

Carson crossed his arms over his chest. "You know, I'm starting to think you just don't want to hang out with me," he said in a playful tone.

Destiny placed a hand against her chest, feigning offense. "What? No, of course not!" She laughed lightly. "Okay fine, you got me. I guess I could clear my very busy, extremely in-demand social calendar for one evening."

Carson's face lit up. "Yeah? Fantastic!"

Destiny winked and shrugged. "What can I say, this town's roads are tricky, I can't let you get lost on the way to the hotel out there."

Destiny donned her favorite red parka, the faux fur trimmed hood framing her face perfectly. She pulled on her trusty Ugg boots, the shearling lining hugging her feet with instant warmth. A chunky knit hat with a fluffy pom pom perched jauntily atop her chestnut waves completed the ensemble.

Her cat Velvet chirped approvingly, purring as she rubbed against Destiny's leg.

Laughing, Destiny scooped up the affectionate tabby and headed for the door. "Let's go!"

Outside, Destiny slid behind the wheel of her reliable old SUV while Velvet curled up on the passenger seat. Carson waited nearby, leaning casually against the sleek rental sedan he'd been driving. He gave Destiny an appreciative nod as she pulled up beside him, amused admiration crinkling the corners of his eyes.

"Nice hat," he teased.

"Why thank you, kind sir," Destiny returned with an exaggerated bow. "Now follow me, and I'll show you the way to Christmas Central."

Carson grinned and hopped into his vehicle. Together they wound through the glowing streets of Christmas Hills, passing shops adorned with twinkling lights. An elaborate Nativity scene dominated the town square, the holy figures dusted with powdery snow.

Velvet purred contentedly, nestled in heat radiating through the seat warmer as Destiny's SUV rounded a corner. They were passing the last cluster of shops and leaving the central district of Christmas Hills behind as they turned onto a winding mountain road leading towards the resort. Snow-dusted pines lined the route, standing sentinel over the pavement. Velvet perked up in her seat, peering out with her paws on the window as a pair of does and a fawn emerged from the trees to watch the passing vehicles.

As Destiny glanced in the rearview mirror to ensure Carson still followed behind, the road curved and suddenly the grand timber facade of the Christmas Hills Resort came into view, twinkling lights draping the peaked rooflines like strands of gold and crystal. Warm illumination glowed from within the expansive windows, emanating a welcoming aura.

Just then, a startled yowl erupted from Velvet. Whipping around, Destiny gasped in horror as Carson's rental sedan spun out of control on the icy road.

Chapter Three

Destiny watched in horror as Carson's rental sedan hit a patch of black ice and spun a pirouette in slow motion. Time seemed to slow as the vehicle spun towards the tree line. Destiny slammed her brakes, tires screeching as she watched helplessly. She thought she saw Carson's eyes wide with panic in her rearview mirror, as the sedan slid toward a cotton tree covered in snow and slammed into it nose-first. Destiny braced herself for a deafening crash but instead heard a dull thud and a white noise that lasted a good three seconds as the tree shook.

Heart pounding, Destiny threw her SUV into park and turned the emergency blinkers on. "Oh my god, Carson!" she cried, leaping from the driver's seat. Velvet followed close behind as Destiny sprinted towards the wreckage. She tried to reach the passenger side but found it had been buried by fallen snow from the tree. "Help me Velvet!" Destiny said as she dug the snow. Velvet made some strange diving maneuvers that seemed to help loosen the snow, and Destiny managed to reach in and wrench the door open. "Carson! Are you okay?"

The driver blinked sluggishly. "Destiny?" he mumbled, eyes struggling to focus. "What... what happened?"

Destiny exhaled in shaky relief. "You hit some ice and crashed into a tree. Are you okay?" She squeezed his hand gently.

Carson grimaced, gingerly rotating his shoulders. "I think so. Just got the wind knocked out of me and maybe have a whiplash." He exhaled in relief. "Thanks for digging me out."

Carson extracted himself from the crumpled sedan, standing unsteadily as he turned to Destiny with a shaky grin. "Well, that was exciting," he quipped, though his face was pale.

Destiny hovered close, relief flooding through her as she realized he was unharmed. "I'm glad you're unharmed, can't say the same about your car though," she teased gently.

Carson laughed, though it came out strained. "Guess I should have paid more attention to those icy road signs." He winced as he rotated his neck. "Though I think my neck will be regretting that impact for a while."

Velvet padded up curiously, sniffing at the tree Carson had collided with. Her ears perked up and her tail twitched as she nosed along the bark.

"What's got her so interested?" Carson asked, watching the cat.

Destiny shook her head. "Velvet's observant, she probably notices the cottonwood tree is different than the rest of the firs and pines in the area."

"Hmm, smart little thing. Don't worry about the car, I'll call the rental company and let them deal with it." Carson tried to stretch his back and groaned.

"Are you sure you don't need to go to the hospital and get checked out?"

"I'm fine, really." He nodded to her SUV. "But maybe you should drive the rest of the way?"

"Of course," Destiny laughed, glad to see him in good spirits. "C'mon Velvet, let's go somewhere cozier," she called out for her feline companion.

As Carson limped towards her vehicle, he glanced back at the tree. For a moment, he thought he saw something among the branches, but then it was gone. Strange, he mused. Probably just blurred vision from the crash. With a shrug, he settled into the passenger seat, wincing as his neck spasmed in protest.

The remainder of the drive was short and uneventful. Within minutes, the winding mountain road gave way to a clearing, revealing the grand timber and glass facade of the Christmas Hills Resort nestled at the foot of the soaring peaks. Destiny pulled her jeep to a stop in the parking lot, allowing Carson a moment to take in the sweeping vista as she unzipped a bubble backpack and Velvet hopped inside.

"Welcome to Christmas Hills Resort," she said with a small smile.

Even in the fading evening light, the lodge radiated yuletide charm. Twinkling icicle lights lined the sloped rooftops, matching the luminous trees dotting the grounds. Within the lobby's grand stone hearth, a towering fir adorned with hand-made ornaments and nostalgic ribbons beckoned visitors inside.

As they stepped through the heavy wooden doors, the scents of cinnamon and pine enveloped them in holiday warmth. Carson blinked at the explosion of decor - nutcrackers standing sentry on the reception desk, shimmering garlands winding up banisters, a miniature snow village nestled around the fireplace, and an elaborate toy train rail system displayed in the hotel lobby. Voices mingled with seasonal melodies as families reunited in overstuffed leather chairs near the hearth.

"Destiny, welcome!" called the petite, dark-haired woman working the front desk. Her eyes lit up as she rushed over to embrace Destiny.

"And Carson, what a wonderful surprise to see you here!" she exclaimed. Turning to Destiny, she added, "Carson and I were colleagues at Foster & Smith Advertising Agency years ago."

Carson turned to Remy with a look of surprise. "How do you and Destiny know each other?" he asked.

Remy laughed, her eyes crinkling with amusement. "Oh Carson, you're clearly not from a small town! Here in Christmas Hills, everyone knows everyone."

Destiny grinned and nodded in agreement. "Remy's right. You can't not know everyone growing up here."

"Destiny and I go way back," Remy elaborated. "We were classmates in high school and both worked part-time jobs around town. I'll never forget the summer Destiny waited tables at Maggie's Diner — she was the fastest plate spinner and kept all the customers entertained."

Destiny blushed slightly at the praise. "I did get pretty good at balancing a full tray on one hand." The two women exchanged a nostalgic smile over childhood memories spent in their close-knit community.

Carson chuckled, realization dawning on him. "Well, it all makes sense now. I should've known in a cozy town like this, you'd have history." He felt a pang of wistfulness, comparing this enduring familiarity to his own transient corporate career that kept him perpetually disconnected.

"How on earth did you end up running this place?"

"I married into the Conley family. My husband Seth inherited the resort after his father passed away unexpectedly last year. We had to shut down for renovations and maintenance last year when Seth first inherited the hotel from his father," Remy explained. "There were some issues that needed addressing, so we decided it was best to close for the holidays and reopen this year, better than ever. I've been learning the hospitality business on the fly, but it's a labor of love."

Carson raised his eyebrows, intrigued by this revelation. "So this is your first Christmas back open under the new ownership?" he asked.

Remy nodded, her pixie cut bobbing. "That's right! We wanted to come back with a bang and really wow our guests. I think we've succeeded." She gestured around the grand lobby, which practically glowed with Christmas spirit.

Destiny and Carson followed Remy further into the grand lobby, admiring the twinkling lights and festive ornaments adorning every surface. As Remy cheerfully pointed out details of the decor, Destiny leaned in towards Carson.

"You know, there were always rumors that the real reason this place shut down last year was because of...strange occurrences," she whispered.

Carson's eyes widened with interest. "What kind of strange occurrences?"

Before Destiny could respond, Remy whirled around, having overheard their hushed exchange.

"Oh, you mustn't pay any mind to silly small-town gossip," Remy admonished lightly, though her smile seemed strained. "We simply needed time for renovations, that's all."

Destiny bit her lip, hesitating. Carson watched the silent exchange between the two women curiously.

"Well, it's just that people talked about...unexplained happenings," Destiny finally continued hesitantly. "You know, like objects moving on their own, electronics going haywire. That sort of thing."

Remy waved a hand dismissively. "Minor issues easily explained by the old infrastructure. All taken care of now thanks to the updates."

Yet Carson detected a flicker of doubt in Remy's eyes that contradicted her breezy assurances. His instincts buzzed. There was more to this story.

Sensing Remy's discomfort, Destiny simply nodded. "You're probably right. Just people gossiping and spinning tall tales, as usual, I'm sure."

Carson made a mental note to ask Remy or Destiny more about the past problems later when they had a private moment. For now, he smiled and nodded. "Well, you all have done a phenomenal job getting the resort back up and running for the holidays."

Remy beamed at the compliment. "Thank you! And I'm so glad to have you both here. We're really embracing this year's theme of 'serendipity' here at the resort," Remy noted, gesturing to the elaborately decorated Christmas trees throughout the space. "Notice how our decor highlights unexpected moments of joy?"

Destiny and Carson exchanged a knowing glance. After their own serendipitous meeting, the resort's whimsical charm felt like coming home.

Remy checked her watch and gasped. "Oh my, look at the time! I'm so sorry, but I need to get back to my managerial duties"

She led Carson and Destiny over to a set of large oak double doors. "This is the entrance to our grand dining room. Please enjoy a wonderful meal together, and I hope to see you both at our tree-lighting ceremony later this evening!"

Remy gave them an apologetic smile. "I'm afraid I must run, but it was so lovely to see you both. Destiny, we really must catch up properly while you're in town. And Carson, I'm thrilled you're staying with us and know you'll have a marvelous time."

After quick hugs, Remy hurried off, her pixie cut bouncing as she rushed back to the front desk, already greeting new guests.

Carson held the dining room door open gallantly for Destiny. "Shall we?" he asked with a playful grin.

The stately dining room of the Christmas Hills Resort exuded old-world charm and luxury. An enormous crystal chandelier dominated the space, its countless prisms casting rainbow flecks across the rich wood-paneled walls. Heavy brocade drapes framed tall windows overlooking the snow-dusted evergreens outside. Crisp white linens adorned tables set with fine china and polished silverware that glinted under the chandelier's glow.

As Destiny and Carson were seated by a tuxedoed server, the scents of sage and roasted garlic teased their senses. Destiny perked up as a tall, dark-haired woman emerged from the kitchen, her chef's whites crisply pressed.

"Kari!" Destiny leaped up to embrace the imposing woman with fierce affection.

"There's my little protégé!" Kari enveloped Destiny in a hug smelling of rosemary and warm yeast. She held Destiny by the shoulders, appraising her with pride.

Kari smiled warmly at Destiny as they settled into their seats. "I'm so thrilled you've returned, my dear. This old town just isn't the same without your smiling face."

Velvet let out a loud meow from the bubble backpack perched on the chair. "And I'm happy to see you too, Velvet," Kari added with a laugh.

Destiny grinned back. "I've missed you too, Kari. And I miss working magic in the kitchen with you."

Kari chuckled. "You flatter me too much. But I must admit, your timing tonight is impeccable. I've crafted a meal to restore warmth on these cold winter nights."

Kari proceeded to detail the menu, her arctic eyes flashing. "First, a rich potato leek soup topped with crispy pancetta and chives. Then, braised beef short ribs with fig and balsamic jus liegende, served with roasted fingerlings and brussels sprouts with toasted hazelnuts."

As Kari proceeded to describe the delectable courses, Carson's mouth watered. But he noticed a subtle tension in the chef's smile, a tightness around her arctic blue eyes.

"And for dessert, warm apple cranberry cobbler with rosemary-infused freshly whipped cream." When Kari finished detailing the menu, Destiny jumped in eagerly. "It all sounds incredible, Kari. I can't wait to catch up more, it's been too long."

Kari nodded but glanced back towards the kitchen. "I wish I could linger, but we're dealing with some... issues at the moment. Nothing to worry about," she added hastily, seeing

Destiny's concern. "Just keeping the staff on their toes, you know how it is. But I'm sure we'll have more time to talk soon."

With an apologetic smile, Kari squeezed Destiny's shoulder and slipped away, her white coat billowing behind her. Before disappearing back into the kitchen, she called over her shoulder, "Bon appétit!"

Destiny turned to Carson, eyes sparkling. "Kari's meals are pure magic. I can't wait for you to taste her food!" As they settled in, Destiny regaled Carson with memories of learning from the ingenious yet intimidating chef.

DESTINY SAVORED another spoonful of the rich potato leek soup, letting the velvety broth and crispy pancetta linger on her tongue. "Mmm, this soup is absolute perfection. Kari has truly outdone herself again."

Carson nodded in agreement as he finished his last bite. "The depth of flavor is incredible."

As the server cleared their empty bowls and brought the next course, Carson turned to Destiny. "So tell me more about this place. It seems like you and Remy go way back."

Destiny sprinkled a touch of sea salt onto her forkful of tender beef short ribs. "Remy and I were classmates growing up here in Christmas Hills. We lost touch after high school when I left for college. I only found out she married Seth Conley last year after the renovations."

"Ah yes, the mysterious renovations," Carson said. "Care to enlighten me about what really went on here?"

Destiny smiled mysteriously. "Let's just say the Conley family has owned this resort for over sixty years. And old places like this tend to attract... interesting stories."

Carson raised an eyebrow. "Now you've got me intrigued. I suspect there are more layers to uncover here during my stay."

He leaned forward, his expression earnest. "Speaking of my stay, I wanted to revisit our earlier conversation. I know I joked about the challenge at first, but I'm serious about wanting to rediscover the spirit of Christmas. And I get the sense you could use some holiday cheer too. What do you say we hold each other accountable as Christmas joy partners?"

Destiny considered him thoughtfully as she sipped her wine. It wouldn't be easy, but she could use a fresh perspective this season. She extended her hand across the table. "Alright Carson, you've got yourself a deal. I accept your challenge." Carson grinned and shook her hand firmly. As if on cue, the server arrived with two steaming dishes of apple cranberry cobbler, topped with a cloud of freshly whipped cream.

"Oh my gosh, the rosemary-infused cream on the cobbler is pure genius," Destiny and Carson were enjoying the last few bites of the delectable apple cranberry cobblers when a sudden rattling sound drew their attention. They glanced around the stately dining room, trying to pinpoint the source of the disturbance, while other diners seemed oblivious.

Destiny's gaze landed on the door leading to the kitchen. To her shock, the brass doorknob was violently shaking, the aged door quivering against the frame. Carson followed her stare and froze. The rattling intensified until, with a sharp crack, the knob broke loose and fell to the floor. It rolled across the hardwood boards with a hollow clatter before slowing to a stop near their table.

Destiny and Carson exchanged an uneasy look. The rest of the diners seemed not to have noticed the strange occurrence. Just then, Destiny felt a strong wind blow over several tables in the dining room, sending tablecloths flying. At the same time, they heard yelling come from the kitchen, followed by the loud crash of plates. This time, they were not the only ones who noticed.

Chapter Four

Destiny glanced over at Carson, concern etched on her delicate features as another loud crash sounded from the kitchen.

"That didn't sound good," she said, already rising from her seat. "I should go check on Kari and make sure no one's hurt." Just as Destiny was about to walk away from her table, Kari strode briskly into the dining room, moving with her usual predatory grace despite the chaotic sounds emanating from the kitchen. As she approached the tables nearest the kitchen entrance, her arctic blue eyes flashed intensely.

"Good evening folks, apologies for the ruckus back there," she announced, her voice crisp and authoritative. "Just a little redecorating accident, nothing to fret over."

Kari clapped her hands sharply, summoning a brigade of servers bearing trays of decadent desserts. "Compliments of the house this evening, thank you for your patience and tolerance. Please enjoy these sweet creations while we tidy up."

The servers swiftly distributed the desserts - rich chocolate tortes drizzled with raspberry sauce, apple cranberry crisps steaming gently, and dainty cups of vanilla bean panna cotta topped with glazed figs. Murmurs of appreciation rose from the diners as they sampled the delectable treats.

Kari strode briskly over to Destiny and Carson's table, her sharp features strained beneath a forced smile. As she leaned in close, she turned slightly towards Destiny and said in a barely audible voice, "Keep an eye out at the tree lighting tonight, be careful."

Before Destiny or Carson could respond, Kari spun on her heel, coat tails flaring dramatically as she strode back towards the kitchen. The doors swung shut behind her, muffling the ongoing cacophony of clatters and shouts echoing within.

Destiny half-rose from her seat, craning her neck towards the kitchen entrance. "Maybe I should go help..." she began uncertainly.

But Carson reached out and touched her arm with a reassuring smile. "It's probably best to stay out of the line of fire right now," he suggested. "Kari seems to have things under control."

Settling back down, Destiny picked up her spoon and scooped a bite of the panna cotta. As the creamy dessert melted on her tongue, the sweetness briefly overpowered her curiosity about the strange events transpiring around the resort.

Carson leaned back in his chair, watching as Destiny savored another spoonful of the velvety panna cotta. "So Kari mentioned something about 'redecorating accidents' in the kitchen," he began casually. "The way she so expertly handled it, makes me wonder if this place really does have issues with weird happenings, like you mentioned earlier."

Destiny paused, lowering her spoon as she considered how to respond.

"The official reason the resort closed last winter was for renovations," she continued. "But it was rumored that the real reason was strange activity escalated. Things that scared the staff and couldn't be explained."

"Like what?" Carson raised an eyebrow, intrigued.

Destiny leaned forward, glancing around briefly before responding in a hushed tone. "Well, according to local gossip, things got pretty bizarre here last winter before the resort abruptly shut down. Whispers of supernatural phenomena that went beyond the usual harmless ghost stories."

She took another spoonful of panna cotta, savoring the sweetness thoughtfully. "Rumor has it that in the kitchen, stacks of plates would suddenly crash to the floor as if shoved by an angry poltergeist. And boiling pots of water and broth turned ice cold in an instant, freezing solid right on the stovetops."

Carson's eyebrows shot up as he listened intently. Destiny continued, "The most disturbing one involved food mysteriously disappearing from locked pantries and refrigerators overnight. Almost like something was... feeding. Of course, Kari and the other staff kept it all hushed up to avoid panic. But folks around here knew something unnatural was happening in this resort."

Destiny shivered slightly, rubbing her arms. "I heard Seth had brought in spiritual experts to perform cleansing and blessing rituals before the hotel reopened. But now, it seems like whatever haunts this place isn't entirely at rest." She nodded discreetly towards the kitchen doors.

Carson absorbed this ominous information with a thoughtful frown. "Huh, so you think this place could actually be haunted?"

Destiny gave a noncommittal tilt of her head. "I try to keep an open mind either way. But there haven't been any casualties or major issues. I believe whatever or whoever is behind all this, they're not really malicious. Maybe they are just having some fun."

She took another bite of dessert, savoring the sweetness before adding softly, "Besides, if things do take a dangerous turn, Kari will act. She protects her own."

Carson nodded slowly, glancing towards the kitchen doors. The clanging and muffled shouts had quieted. For now, an air of forced holiday calm settled over the dining room. But an undercurrent of mystery and uncertainty lingered.

OUT IN THE resort's sprawling gardens, a towering pine tree stood ready to be illuminated for the holidays. Strings of lights and countless ornaments adorned the branches, waiting to cast their festive glow across the snow-dusted landscape.

The crowd was going crazy, but Remy had saved them special spots up front, so they weren't in the middle of the chaos. Seth and Remy took the stage beside the pine tree, microphone in hand. Carson glanced at Destiny as she smiled, eyes wide with excitement, and he took her hand.

"Welcome, everyone, to our annual tree lighting ceremony!" Seth's voice boomed across the crowd. "We have a wonderful holiday season in store for you all here at the Christmas Hills Resort."

As he continued speaking about the hotel's festive plans, Remy gazed up at her husband with obvious affection. When Seth finally declared it was time to illuminate the tree, he and Remy together grasped the giant switch. An explosion of glittering colors lit up the pine as the switch was pulled. The crowd cheered and Carson let out an impressed whistle.

"Now doesn't that just get you in the Christmas spirit?" he said, turning to Destiny with a grin. She smiled back, but a flicker of some indiscernible emotion passed through her eyes.

Then the crowd started singing Christmas carols. Destiny's voice was beautiful, rich, and struck a chord within him, but the only lyrics he knew of the song were the parts about the Christmas tree. She tilted her head up and looked at him with a lopsided smile when she noticed his limited repertoire.

"The next thing we are doing for your Christmas joy challenge is to learn a few Christmas songs," Destiny said.

Carson grinned sheepishly. "I guess you could say my holiday playlist is a little lacking. But maybe you can help fix that while we're here."

"I'd be happy to," Destiny said, playfully nudging his arm. "We'll have to start with the classics, like Rudolph the Red-Nosed Reindeer, had a very shiny nose?"

"Now that one I do know!" Carson exclaimed. He didn't know why he did it, but he perched his nose on hers. "Kind of like yours in this cold," he teased, then pulled away.

"Destiny! I thought that was you."

"Ugh," Destiny's cheeks flushed pink, and he dropped his hand to turn to the woman who approached. "Mom!" Her mom took her in for a quick hug, but the woman's eyes never left Carson.

"Well, what do we have here?" Diane asked, eyebrow raised knowingly as she looked between Destiny and Carson.

Destiny quickly stepped back, brushing a strand of hair behind her ear self-consciously. "I didn't realize you were coming to the ceremony. Is Dad here?"

"We wouldn't miss it! Your Dad just went to get a hot cocoa." Diane replied. She turned her shrewd gaze to Carson. "And who might this young man be?"

"Hi, I'm Carson Akin, ma'am," he said, extending his hand politely. Had she seen them touching noses?

"Carson's a... friend, of Remy's," Destiny added hastily. "We just met today."

Diane's eyes glinted. "Is that so? Well, it's wonderful to meet one of Destiny's friends."

Destiny shifted uncomfortably, anxiety rising at her mother's implications. "Anyway, I'm off to show him Snowman Alley and the observatory. See you later!"

"Have fun," her mom cooed." She touched Carson's arm.

Carson nodded, picking up on her eagerness to escape. "That sounds perfect." He gave Diane a polite parting smile. "It was nice to meet you, Mrs. Mellowes."

"You as well, Carson," Diane replied knowingly. "I'm sure I'll be seeing you again soon."

Destiny quickly led Carson away through the dispersing crowd, relieved to avoid further meddling from her mother. Once far enough away, she let out a tense laugh. "Sorry about that. My mom can be a bit... overbearing sometimes. Should we try our hand at making a snowman?" she asked."

“Yes, but I’ve got to admit, this would be my first time.”

She grabbed his hand. “It’s been a long time for me too. Come on.” They walked through a maze, stopping to grab sticks, mittens, and carrots from a pile. By the time they found a spot to stop, both their hands were full. She laughed as she dropped her heap of snowman-building material near her feet. “We might have overdone it.”

He kneeled on his knee and grabbed a bunch of snow. They ended up making two larger-sized and three smaller-sized, all dressed but deformed. One had earrings hanging off lopsided ears, one’s nose was closer to the eyes than the center, and the one with earrings had a huge bottom and middle portion with a very small head. He stepped back, and she grabbed her phone to snap photos.

“Come on, we’ve got to get this on camera. It’s evidence that you have found your Christmas joy.”

She snapped a few, and he waved her over. “Come on, we can get some selfies.” They took a few together, then laughed at the contorted figures. Carson patted one of the snowmen with his gloved hands. “I believe this little lady is about to pop with a snow baby.”

“Oh my gosh, Carson You are hilarious!” She fell laughing into the soft powder near the snow family and glanced at the stars. Snowman Alley was sectioned off with a wooden fence strung with bright white LED lights. All the trees surrounding the area twinkled with lights of many colors. The sprinkling stars melding with the decorations sent a warm current into her heart and for a moment, she remembered all the joys of Christmases past. She stood up and brushed the snow off of her.

. . .

"ARE you ready to check out the observatory?" Her entire body tingled, vibration high as she walked with him to the observatory. Inside the domed building, they looked at the stars, and he was amazed to see Saturn's rings and the deep moon craters. Destiny had forgotten how much she enjoyed any of this. It had been a long time.

Afterward, they strolled over to one of the many outdoor fire pits scattered around the resort, settling into the cozy Adirondack chairs beside the flickering flames. Two Clydesdale horses pulling a red carriage carried a laughing couple through a path lined with lighted trees.

"I've never taken a horse carriage ride, either."

"That's definitely something we need to add to the list." She pointed near a building with a long line. "But I say we wait to do that another day, because that's the line, and they've already signed up."

"Oh wow, okay. You know what else I've never done?"

"What's that?" she asked.

"Sipped hot cocoa by a warm fire."

"I know the perfect place for that."

She led him to the festive booth that served hot cocoa, hot apple cider, and spiced mulled wine. They each opted for a cup of hot cocoa, served with a peppermint bark stirrer. Then they walked towards the outdoor fires. People were gathered around the large fire, but many smaller fires in pits were spread throughout the area. The band had been replaced with Christmas carolers, and their voices streamed throughout the speakers. Many joined along, so they found a quiet place near the ice skating rink.

Carson tipped his head toward the rink. “That’s something else I’ve never really done. Okay, maybe once or twice, but I can’t say I’m any good at it.”

“Another thing to add to your list! You’ll go back to work bursting with Christmas joy!”

“It’s like destiny,” he said. Her ears perked at his low voice, and she narrowed her eyes. “What?”

His gaze lingered over her, warming her. “Meeting you. Being here with you. I already found some joy in all of it. There’s no way I could do this without you. I’d already be going crazy.”

“Is it because of too much Christmas music?” she asked, joking.

He laughed. “Too much Christmas, period. But no. How could I have enjoyed the whole snowman-building thing if you weren’t here?”

Destiny took out her phone, swiping through the photos they had taken together in Snowman Alley. She smiled at the silly selfies they had snapped, making silly faces at the camera. But then she came to the pictures of their snowmen creations and froze.

She vividly remembered sculpting whimsical smiles on the lopsided snowmen’s faces. Yet now in the photos, their features were distorted into gaping, sinister grimaces. Destiny stared at the photos, a chill running down her spine. She was certain those pleasant smiles had been there in real life just moments ago. What could explain the eerie, ominous faces now captured on her phone? She quickly clicked past the snowman pictures, not wanting Carson to see.

"Oh wow, is it really that late already?" she said. She tucked her phone back into her pocket and stood up from the cozy

Adirondack chairs they had settled into by the firepit. "I need to get going."

Carson studied her face, sensing something seemed off about her sudden hurry to leave. "Is everything okay?"

She finally met Carson's gaze again with a tight smile that didn't quite reach her eyes. “Yeah, it’s just late. We can continue the challenge tomorrow, okay? Enjoy the rest of your night."

Before Carson could respond, Destiny had already turned and started walking briskly back toward the resort's main building. Carson watched her retreating figure, perplexed by her abrupt change in demeanor.

Destiny hurried home, her mind spinning. The cheerful night had taken such an unsettling turn. Those ominous snowman faces haunted her, impossible to explain yet undeniably real.

As Destiny collapsed onto the bed, Velvet gave a small mew and crawled onto Destiny's chest, kneading her paws contentedly as Destiny stroked her soft fur. Destiny's thoughts drifted back to Carson. He had seemed so charming and fun initially. But now she recalled his nickname at work - Satan. A chill went through her. What if there was a darker side to him that she couldn't yet see? Velvet purred, pulling her from her doubts. Destiny sighed and cuddled the cat close. "You're right girl, I'm probably overthinking this. He seems like a decent guy. But I'd better stay cautious until I know him better."

Destiny yawned, the excitement of the day catching up with her. Tomorrow she could try and make sense of it all. For now, she needed rest. She curled up under the covers, Velvet nestled cozily at her side, and let her eyes drift shut.

Chapter Five

The morning sunlight filtering through the frosted window panes stirred Destiny awake. She languished under the cozy covers as the events of the last day replayed in her mind - the intriguing encounters with Carson, the strange occurrences around town, and the brewing excitement of the holidays.

Destiny rolled over to grab her phone from the nightstand and saw an unread text message from Carson. "Good morning! I wanted to thank you for humoring me yesterday. You're never going to believe this, but there was a Christmas tree in my room when I got back last night. I think Remy must have had someone come in and decorate while we were out making snowmen. Let me know if you'd be interested in getting a tree today. I could use an authentic tree-shopping experience. Plus it's a good excuse to see you again."

She chuckled. Remy, the queen of Christmas, would ensure all her guests had the best experience ever. And this worked out perfectly because now they would have more time to decorate her home, if he wanted to help that is.

"I was thinking I needed a tree for my house, maybe even lights, if you're up for helping?"

He was quick to respond. "Absolutely!"

She took a breath and texted back, "How about breakfast first? I can meet you at the resort at eight?"

"I'll be waiting!"

His quick agreement sent her pulse racing in anticipation and she rushed to the resort, nearly giddy with excitement.

Carson was on the lobby couch when she arrived.

"Well good morning, fancy meeting you here," he greeted her.

"Fancy indeed, did you sleep well?" Destiny smiled.

"I actually did. The room is great. You?"

She nodded, not admitting she had tossed and turned thinking about him and all the strange occurrences.

"So now that you have your tree sorted, are you ready to help me pick one out from the farm?" Destiny changed the topic.

"Yes, I can't wait."

She watched his reaction closely for any hint of discomfort and noticed only genuine excitement. He smiled, "Let's see what the chef has in store for us this morning. I'm going to need a hearty breakfast if I'm going to be chopping trees later."

Before they reached the grand oak doors, Remy burst out looking distressed. She halted upon seeing them, smoothing down her hair and tidying her rumpled blouse.

"Oh! Hello... I was just, uh, taking care of something," Remy muttered hastily. She shook her head and attempted a smile that came out as more of a grimace. Carson raised an eyebrow.

"Well we won't keep you, but thank you again for the tree you left in my room," he said politely.

"Yes of course, happy to spread the holiday cheer," Remy replied, though she blinked hard as if just remembering. "You two enjoy your breakfast."

With that, she rushed off down the hall. Destiny watched her disappear around a corner, frowning.

"Now what do you suppose that was about?" she mused. Carson held the door open, gesturing for her to enter the dining hall first.

"No clue, but clearly she has her hands full keeping this place running smoothly," he replied.

Inside the dining hall, the tantalizing aroma of maple and baked cinnamon greeted them. Destiny inhaled deeply. Oak tables were laden with heaps of bacon, sausage, pancakes, bowls of fresh fruit, and trays of gourmet pastries. A server offered them warm mulled wine.

Destiny sipped her wine as she and Carson filled their plates and settled at a table by the soaring windows. Velvety snowflakes drifted down outside. Destiny sliced into a stack of gingerbread pancakes drizzled with bourbon pecan syrup, sighing contentedly at her first sweet, nutty bite.

"Quite the spread," Carson said before sampling a cinnamon bun.

"Mm, it's delicious. Kari outdid herself," Destiny nodded. Between tasty mouthfuls, they chatted lightly about their plans for the tree farm. Halfway through the meal Kari herself emerged from the kitchen.

"There are my favorite customers," she exclaimed, giving Destiny a quick hug. "You both look rather cozy this morning," she added with a wink.

Destiny felt her cheeks flush. "We were just discussing heading to the farm next."

"How festive! Well, I expect details on this little outing later," Kari said. She leaned down and squeezed Destiny's shoulder. "I need to get back to the kitchen. But find me after, we should catch up."

After Kari bustled off, Destiny set down her utensils.

"Have you noticed anything else strange going on here at the resort?" she asked Carson. "Remy seemed quite flustered earlier."

Carson's expression clouded briefly. "I wish I knew. Though it certainly seems like they're dealing with something odd." He straightened up, smiling again. "Shall we get going?"

THE SNOW GLITTERED under late morning sunlight as Destiny and Carson wandered the rows of towering firs at the Christmas Hills Tree Farm. They passed countless tipi-shaped wooden stands displaying assorted wreaths, garlands, and candles. The scent of fresh pine hung deliciously in the chilled air. Destiny brushed her mittened fingers over the needled branches as she examined each tree.

Near the back row, a massive fifteen-foot fir caught her attention. Its symmetrical shape and full greenery begged to be decorated. Carson let out an impressed whistle.

"Quite the specimen. Should we take this one?" He grinned, clearly joking. But Destiny tilted her head, picturing it glowing with lights and ornament in her living room.

“Whoa, I was thinking of something around six feet, 8 feet max. But you know what, let's do it!" she declared with a laugh. Carson blinked in surprise.

Just then the tree farm manager, MacGregor, came lumbering over. His ruddy cheeks nearly matched his red plaid shirt.

"Can I help ye folks with somethin’?” he bellowed in his Scottish burr. Destiny indicated the towering fir.

"We'd love to take this one off your hands," she said.

MacGregor let loose a hearty guffaw. “That tree's taller than my cottage! But lemme get the saw if you’re sure about it." Still chuckling, he went to grab the equipment.

Moments later Carson stood with gloves and goggles on, saw in hand, sizing up their prize. Destiny clasped her mittened hands together, bouncing excitedly on her toes.

"You aren’t getting cold feet now are you?” she teased. Carson scoffed.

“Please, just sit back and watch how it’s done.”

He set the jagged teeth against the truck and pushed forward forcefully. But the blade barely bit into the weathered bark. Carson repositioned, throwing his weight behind the saw, his breath coming out in frosted puffs. After what seemed an eternity, a section of the trunk finally splintered away.

“Progress!” Carson huffed triumphantly. But glancing up, he frowned at all the work left. Shaking out his numb fingers, he doggedly hacked on. Logs and piles of pine needles accumulated around his feet.

As Destiny laughed encouragingly, her phone jangled loudly. Pulling it from her coat pocket she saw it was Kari. Ducking behind a nearby tent, she swiped the screen.

"Kari? Is everything okay?"

On the other end, Kari replied in a hushed voice. "Hey Des. We found something at the hotel this morning. One of the vacant rooms looking like a frozen wasteland. Frost coating every surface. The thermostat was turned up full blast. No rational explanation whatsoever!"

Destiny gasped. What was going on at that resort? As she recounted yesterday's peculiar events - the grinning snowmen, the wind that swept through the dining room when all the windows were closed, the rattling doorknob that suddenly fell to the floor as if it was a decapitated head. Destiny remembered the odd run-in with Remy earlier. "How strange! No wonder Remy was in a hurry when we saw her this morning. She must've been in the middle of putting out this fire. Um, no pun intended."

Kari chuckled appreciatively, "Des, I'm not sure if there's anything to this, but I think you should know, that the frozen room is right across from Carson's." She exhaled heavily across the line. "I'm having some problems in my kitchen too, it all started yesterday, and Carson is in the center of all this strangeness. I want you to keep an eye on him, can you do that?"

Just then Destiny spotted Carson wrestling through the muddy slush with the massive tree. Grunting with effort, he heaved it towards MacGregor's wrapping station.

"I hear you, Kari. We ran into some inexplicable stuff last night too. I'm with him at the tree farm right now so I can't really talk. But I'll see what else I can learn."

They said hurried goodbyes just as Carson caught sight of her. His cheeks flushed from exertion, resembling an exuberant lumberjack. Destiny smiled and shook her head in amusement. What secrets could he be hiding behind that disarming smile?

She hurried out of the tent and ran up to him. "Yay! We have a tree."

He grunted, "Yeah. Now let's see if this thing will fit in that Jeep of yours."

"I'll help carry it, at least." Each taking an end, they carried it to the farm entrance where MacGregor's sons took over, shaking it out and netting it while MacGregor handled payment and extras like a tree stand.

"Want something to drink while they get the tree ready?" MacGregor asked.

"I'm not sure I could handle anything hot right now," Carson admitted.

"I have Coca-Cola and tea, and ice too."

"Coke sounds wonderful."

"I'll take a hot cocoa," Destiny said.

"Coming right up."

While they waited, Destiny high-fived him and said, "That was fun to watch."

"What? Watching me struggle with a giant tree?" Her eyes gleamed while she accepted the to-go mug from MacGregor.

She smiled. "MacGregor's sons would've helped."

"And take away all the fun? No way."

After MacGregor finished binding the tree to Destiny's jeep, the pair headed back into town to shop for ornaments. Rustic glass bulbs, velvet bows, and regal wise men soon filled their bags. They debated festive versus elegant decor combinations over sandwiches at a corner bakery. For a moment the resort's odd events faded from Destiny's mind.

"We can keep this up until we drop, but I honestly think we have enough ornaments for now. I'm eager to go home and start decorating."

Carson nodded, finishing his sandwich. "Sounds great. I need to do one thing — won't take long. Meet you back here in five minutes?" She narrowed her eyes but said nothing. He stood up and strode out the door without another word.

What was that about? She leaned sideways trying to spot where he went, but he had already disappeared from view. Her conversation with Kari came flooding back.

An hour later, arms laden with shopping bags, Destiny opened her front door. Velvet immediately dashed over, purring loudly as she encircled the humans who just walked in, tail waving like a festive banner.

"Aren't you lucky you got to stay home all nice and cozy!" Destiny hunched down and hugged Velvet.

They went back to the jeep after dropping all their bags and wrestled the tree free. A few minutes later, the splendid fir they had worked so hard procuring dominated her cozy living room.

Carson stepped up behind her, his cheeks still ruddy from the cold. "Shall we commence decorating m'lady?" He held up a bag of shiny round bulbs.

"Absolutely, kind sir!" Destiny agreed, hoping her smile didn't seem too forced. Selecting a Hall and Oates Christmas album, she soon lost herself in seasonal revelry. Time faded away as they draped twinkling lights, tied crimson velvet bows, and hung colorful glass ornaments from every bough.

About halfway through, Carson halted, snapping his gloved fingers. "Shoot, I think I left one of my ornament bags in your car earlier. Be right back!"

Before Destiny could respond he disappeared outside again. She watched his retreating figure through the window with a furrowed brow.

Glancing down, she spotted the wool coat he had flung over the sofa in the living room. On impulse she moved towards it, curiosity getting the best of her. She reached into the left pocket and fished his leather wallet out. A few credit cards... nothing remarkable there. She reached into the right pocket and was pleased to find the photo of the beautifully unique art deco ring that she printed out for him when they first met. He had kept it as a good luck charm as he said he would.

Digging deeper into the right pocket, she felt her fingers close on something flat, and cold. Pulling it out revealed a flat metal object in the shape of an avocado, with circular cutouts in various places. Destiny studied it with furrowed brows, having no guesses as to its purpose. She grabbed her cell phone, quickly snapping some photos of it.

Just then the doorknob turned, causing her to jump. She quickly shoved both items back into Carson's pockets, ran to the tree, and started hanging up ornaments.

Carson returned grinning, producing several glittering antique bulb ornaments. "Got 'em! Sorry, didn't mean to leave you hanging."

He strode forward and Destiny plastered on a smile. "No worries! Those are gorgeous," she managed.

They carried on decorating in awkward silence for several minutes and were nearly finished with the tree's decorations when she realized she had no idea where her tree topper might be — a sparkling crystal star from her childhood. Carson cleared his throat just as her mind raced to remember.

"Well, I wanted this to be a surprise for later. But I thought, why not make it your tree topper..."

He revealed a beautifully crafted angel, her porcelain face serene, wispy blonde hair flowing about her shoulders. Her white lace gown and feathered wings were accented in gold. Destiny caught her breath.

"Oh my goodness, she's lovely!"

He lifted the angel above Destiny's head, gently fitting her atop the massive fir. Destiny looked at the finished project, the tree now complete with its adornments and shining starry guardian. Unexpected emotion caught in her throat.

"It's absolutely perfect," she whispered.

She turned back to see Carson watching her. Behind the ad exec facade, she thought she spotted a deep well of caring and vulnerability he kept hidden away. Like there might be much more to this man than met the eye.

"Do you want to stay for dinner? I can throw something together for us. As a small thanks," Destiny offered gently, feeling guilty for doubting him and going through his things while all he did was go to the car to get her a present.

“Dinner sounds lovely, I’d love to stay.”

Soon the cozy kitchen was filled with sizzling herbs, diced vegetables, and the simmering scents of Destiny's signature pasta sauce. Carson sat at the counter, sipping a glass of Barolo as Destiny bustled about. She artfully layered noodles, sauce, buffalo mozzarella, and parmesan then slid the baking dishes into the oven.

Twenty minutes later she cut two perfect squares and plated them with a flourish. Steam rose, releasing an indulgently rich aroma. Carson's eyes grew round as Destiny set down the meals with a Caesar salad and toasted baguette slices.

"For you sir. Homemade lasagna Florentine with spinach, ricotta, Italian sausage, mushrooms, my secret sauce... " She raised her glass of wine towards him.

Carson took an eager bite, chewing slowly with his eyes closed. "Mmm... oh my God that's incredible,” he mumbled through the mouthful. He swallowed, shaking his head in awe.

"Seriously Destiny, you could open your own restaurant with skills like this. Have you ever considered it?"

Destiny lowered her fork, hesitation clouding her face. Since childhood she had dreamed of studying culinary arts abroad, backpacking through Tuscan wineries, and visiting Michelin-star kitchens. Instead, she had taken some detours in life and returned to the family framing business to help her parents. Though she adored cooking, the aspiration of becoming a renowned chef now seemed buried in the past.

Sensing her inner conflict, Carson set down his utensils and met her gaze.

"Hey, it's obvious you've got serious talent. I know potential when I see it. If you ever want advice on turning that passion into a business, my offer stands. I'd be happy to help."

Warm appreciation flooded through Destiny at his words. The fact someone practical like Carson saw such capability within her lit a small flame inside that had wavered for too long. She opened her mouth to thank him but was interrupted by Velvet leaping onto the counter.

"Velvet!" Destiny scolded. But instead of the lasagna, the little cat made a beeline for Carson. She gracefully trotted over, purring loudly as she nuzzled under his hand. Carson blinked in astonishment as he gave her chin a stroke.

"Well, what do you know? It took months before she'd go near my last boyfriend," Destiny said in wonderment.

Velvet continued head-butting Carson insistently until he scooped her up. She snuggled into his sweater without hesitation. Carson chuckled.

"What can I say, I have a way with the ladies." He winked at Destiny as he cuddled the contented cat like an old friend.

Over espressos and snickerdoodles a bit later, she listened intently as Carson described different online package options for showcasing her work digitally - logos, photos, video episodes of the Destiny Mellowes cooking show.

By the time she waved goodnight to Carson's retreating figure over an hour later, she was laden with conflicted emotions, her suspicions about him now clashing with his show of genuine support for her. If she kept prying, would she uncover sinister secrets about this appealing mystery man? Or perhaps hidden depths of compassion and care instead? Destiny sighed, moving to sit on her living room floor beside the tree they had brought home together. The angel he had gifted her gazed down, holding her secrets for the time being.

Chapter Six

Destiny hurried through the maze of stainless steel counters and towering ovens, the hotel kitchen clanging with lunch rush mayhem. Savory aromas of shallot and white wine tickled her nose from an enormous pot of French onion soup destined for the dining room. She spotted Kari amidst the controlled chaos, sharply directing her staff of line cooks like a grand orchestra conductor.

"Kari! Got a minute?" Destiny called over sizzling skillets.

Kari signaled for her to follow to a quieter prep area and started artfully peeling a small mountain of potatoes. "Talk to me."

"I spied on Carson, Kari. I don't feel good about it, but I did it." Destiny pulled out her phone and showed Kari the photo she had taken of the strange metal object. "I found this in his coat pocket. Any idea what it is?"

Kari peered closely at the image. "That's a planchette," she said after a moment. "A cheap, mass-produced one from the looks of it. See that tiny 'Made in China' stamped on the side?"

Destiny nodded, zooming in on the photo. The inscription was nearly invisible to the naked eye.

"Planchettes are used with Ouija boards for communicating with spirits," Kari explained, expertly slicing potatoes. "Though most sold nowadays are just novelty items. Sometimes even as keychains in souvenir shops."

"So why would Carson have one?" Destiny wondered aloud.

Kari arched an eyebrow. "That is peculiar. Especially given the... happenings around here lately." She directed a meaningful look Destiny's way.

"Could you enlighten me further regarding these planchettes?" Destiny questioned.

"I come from a long line of Icelandic mystics. My forebears practiced two forms of magic - Galdur, utilized by men, and Seiðr, confined to women."

"Like witchery?" Destiny asked interestedly.

"Yes," Kari responded. "Seiðr, the form that women practiced, entailed channeling spirits for divination and clairvoyance. When we want to talk to spirits, talk to the dead, we let their voices come through us, possess us, in a way. It can be dangerous, depending on the spirit we are trying to contact and depending on the witch. The planchette operates in a similar way, except, it allows the spirit to spell or write through this object, instead of speaking through the vocal cords of witches. It's a safer way to concentrate energy and connect with entities beyond the veil, think of it like, channeling-lite."

Destiny shivered, simultaneously intrigued by Kari's magical background and disturbed by her revelation regarding the object in Carson's pocket.

"Do you think Carson could be conjuring up ghosts or something?" Destiny asked nervously.

"I'm not sure yet," Kari replied. "But Remy and I were just discussing how all this spooky activity seemed to have started when Carson arrived in town."

Destiny nodded slowly, her stomach knotting with apprehension.

"In fact," Kari continued, "I just spoke to Remy, she said she's going to put Carson through the Benson test, tonight." A knowing glint flashed in her pale eyes.

"What's the Benson test?" Destiny pressed.

"You'll see. Let's just say if Carson isn't who he claims to be, Benson will know."

Destiny frowned, puzzled by the cryptic reference.

Kari patted Destiny's shoulder reassuringly. "I know you like him. Don't worry, if he's good, he's good. If he isn't, you don't want him as a friend anyway. It'll all be revealed soon."

REMY WAS MAKING her way down the grand corridor of the Christmas Hills Resort when she spotted Carson headed in the opposite direction.

"Carson! I'm so glad I ran into you," Remy called out in her melodic voice. Carson turned and gave her a friendly smile as she approached. Though they had only worked briefly together at the ad agency, Remy's gregarious nature allowed her to form quick connections.

"Remy, nice to see you again," Carson responded warmly. "How are things at the resort today?"

"Oh, you know, the usual chaos trying to pull off a perfect holiday season, never a dull moment!" Remy said, a barely detectable tension in her voice.

"And what about you? Are you getting into the Christmas spirit yet?"

Carson chuckled. "I'm working on it. This place definitely makes it easier with all the festivities." He hesitated before continuing. "And honestly, Destiny's really been helping to inspire me. She's a talented chef, did you know that?"

"How wonderful!" Remy clapped her hands together eagerly. "Destiny is a real talent in the kitchen. And so passionate about food. I'd love to see her succeed."

Carson nodded enthusiastically. "She's amazing in the kitchen. The way she handles ingredients and flavors, it's like magic. I really think she could make it big with the right resources and exposure." He went on to describe his vision for creating promotional videos showcasing Destiny's skills and unique culinary creations. Remy listened intently, smiling at Carson's obvious admiration for Destiny's talents.

"It sounds like you two really connect on a creative level," Remy observed. "And I agree - Destiny has such a gift! With your marketing expertise, I'm sure you could help amplify her brand beautifully."

"I just want to see her achieve her dreams, you know? She deserves it." Carson's eyes twinkled with purpose as he considered the possibilities.

Remy paused as if she was seized by a sudden idea. "You know, you should both join my husband Seth and me for dinner this evening.

I'd love to introduce you properly, and Destiny can tell us more about her goals. Seth has all kinds of connections in the industry."

Carson looked surprised but pleased by the invitation. "That's incredibly kind of you, Remy. I'm sure Destiny would be thrilled at the opportunity. Let me invite her."

"Perfect!" Remy gave him an approving nod. "It's settled then. We'll see you later tonight, say at seven o'clock? Now if you'll excuse me, I need to go put out some fires."

With a wave, Remy glided off, leaving Carson excited at the prospect of helping Destiny's dreams materialize over this serendipitous dinner.

DESTINY PICKED AT HER FOOD, lost in thought amidst the friendly chatter between Remy, Seth, and Carson over dinner at the grand dining room of the Christmas Hills Resort. She glanced up occasionally, mustering a faint smile, but her mind kept drifting back to Kari's ominous words.

"Enjoying your stay?" Seth asked.

"It's very nice."

Seth chewed. "Really? Tell us more?”

"Honestly, I’m beginning to feel the Christmas essence in my bones."

He looked at Destiny, who quickly looked away. He wondered what was up.

Seth rubbed his hands. "So Remy told me about you wanting to help Destiny's culinary career or something like that. How’s that coming along?"

Carson leaned back in his chair, looking thoughtful as he considered Seth's question. "Well, I had a few ideas for helping Destiny get her culinary business off the ground. The first step is building her a great website to showcase her talents and start taking orders. I was thinking we could really play up the whole 'small town chef making homecooked meals with love' angle. Lots of photos of Destiny cooking, images of the finished dishes beautifully plated..."

He glanced over at Destiny, who was still staring at her plate and oddly disinterested. Carson continued, "Beyond the website, we could produce some short cooking videos to share on social media - TikTok, Instagram, YouTube. Simple stuff filmed on a phone to start. The goal is getting Destiny's personality and passion for food to shine through."

Destiny smiled softly at that, envisioning herself as a social media cooking star.

Remy leaned towards Seth and whispered, "I told you he's good at this."

Seth nodded approvingly. "You seem to have solid ideas there. Once the website and videos get traction, the resort would be happy to place bulk orders for catering events and in-room dining!"

He took a sip of wine, then added, "If you need any help getting the word out locally, just ask. I assure you news travels fast here, which is great except when it's not. Trust me, I know this personally." He said as he glanced at Remy, who tried to suppress a laugh, obviously in on the inside joke.

The maître d' approached their table and tapped Seth on the shoulder. "Now if you'll excuse me for a moment," Seth said as he stood up and walked away, only to return with a small dog no bigger than Velvet a moment later. He was covered in long black fur and wearing a red bow tie. Destiny thought there was something familiar about him but couldn't put a finger on it.

"Who's this little guy?" Carson jumped on the chance to change the subject.

"This is Benson," the little dog addressed everyone by looking them each in the eye, his gaze lingering longer on Carson. Finally, he looked away and then settled on Seth's lap.

Remy exhaled as Destiny finally smiled. Carson had passed the Benson test. He wasn't behind the strange phenomena after all.

"Am I missing something here?" Carson asked.

"Benson was a gift from my father. Ever since he was little, he's exhibited some uncanny talent. I didn't believe it at first, but he's helped us identify people with ill intent and even helped catch thieves in the past. He's our little truth detector." Seth introduced proudly.

"What a great little guy you are! I'm sorry, I still feel like I'm missing something?" Carson asked again.

Remy went on to explain, starting with the strange phenomena that started happening at the hotel around the time Carson arrived.

Carson looked over at Destiny, who was staring at the table. He felt hurt but didn't fail to see the humor in the situation. "You guys thought I was the one behind the wind, the rattling doorknob, and the plates smashing in the kitchen? I'm flattered." He said in a stern voice, but couldn't hide his smile.

Destiny finally released the breath she had been holding, relieved to see he wasn't angry that they suspected him.

"Carson, we knew it wasn't you, but had to make sure before we pursued the other theory," Remy said.

"What's the other theory?"

Remy and Seth looked at one another then book shook their heads. "Still too early to say."

"Does it have anything to do with wayward spirits?"

"Where did you get that idea?"

"Santa Pat gave me some advice. He said something about 'having to communicate with what perturbs you when things start to get weird' and gave me something to help me communicate with 'it', whatever 'it' is."

"Seems the news is making more waves than we think," Remy said with a worried expression.

Seth patted her back. "We'll figure it out, honey."

"What did he give you?"

"Some kind of metallic thing with patterns and holes on it."

Carson reached into his coat pocket and pulled out the thin, metallic object that Santa Pat had gifted him. He placed it on the table for the others to examine.

"What in the world is that thing?" Seth asked as he picked it up and turned it over in his hands.

Remy leaned in for a closer look. "A new type of bottle opener?"

Destiny shifted uncomfortably in her seat. "It is a planchette," she said quietly.

The others turned to look at her. "How do you know that?" Remy asked.

Destiny glanced down, avoiding their gazes. "Because... I saw it earlier. When I went through Carson's coat pocket."

"You went through my coat?" Carson asked in surprise.

"I'm sorry," Destiny said, her cheeks flushing pink with embarrassment. "It's just... with all the strange things happening, I was starting to have some doubts and I thought maybe you were behind it all. So when you left your coat at my place, I looked through the pockets and found that thing."

"Why would you think I was behind it all?" Carson asked gently.

Destiny fidgeted with her napkin. "Honestly? It seemed like the weird stuff started right around the time you got into town. And you told me your nickname was 'Satan' at work..."

Carson couldn't help it - he burst out laughing uncontrollably. "Oh, that?" he said between laughs. "You really think I would tell you my nickname was Satan if I was really evil?"

Destiny's face flushed an even deeper red. She abruptly stood up from the table. "I'm sorry, I have to go." She hurried out of the dining room.

Carson was stunned at the turn of events.

“Wait, Destiny, I promise there's nothing sinister about it. Just an office joke because I don't get into the Christmas spirit." He said, jumping up to go after her.

REMY and Seth sat in silence at the table as Destiny rushed out and Carson hurried after her. They exchanged a look.

"I suppose we must acknowledge the elephant in the room," Seth said quietly. "It seems we can avoid it no longer - our beloved resort may be haunted again."

Remy sighed, sadness and resignation in her eyes. "You're right. We can't ignore the signs anymore."

Seth took a long sip of his wine, his hand trembling ever so slightly as he set the glass back down. "I can't help but think of my father's strange behavior those last few months," he shook his head. "I thought it was just his health getting worse. But now..." His voice trailed off and he rubbed a hand over his weary face.

"If there really is something supernatural happening here again, we'll need to get to the bottom of it quickly. Before word spreads and our reputation is damaged." Seth's tone turned urgent. "We have to protect my father's legacy, and the future of this resort."

CARSON RETURNED TO HIS ROOM, frustration simmering after his failed attempt to catch up with Destiny. The evening had taken an unexpectedly humiliating turn for them both.

Stepping into his suite, Carson winced as his foot landed on a loose floorboard, emitting an obnoxious squeak. In his agitated state, the noise grated on his nerves. Glaring at the offending board, he dragged the Christmas tree over to cover it.

With the squeak muffled, his OCD sated, Carson felt a sense of satisfaction. He started rearranging the rest of the furniture in his room around the relocated tree, channeling his restless energy into optimizing the layout, occasionally stepping back to admire his adjustments. As he worked, Carson's perspective began to shift. Destiny's prying stung, yet he'd laughed thoughtlessly, escalating the awkwardness.

Amidst this holiday havoc, he had gained self-awareness. Just like this room, his view required fresh eyes.

Chapter Seven

Remy and Seth stumbled into the bustling kitchen, weaving slightly from the wine they had with dinner. Around them, a bizarre scene unfolded with Kari and her brigade in an exercise in organized chaos, as flames leaped, pans sizzled, and knives in various hands chopped out a polyrhythmic tempo.

"Kari, darling!" Remy sang out above the clamor. The chef spared her a glance, hands busy seasoning two dishes at once.

"We must discuss the situation," Seth declared, leaning against the stainless steel counter. He lurched back as a sous chef whisked the cutting board from under him.

Kari waved them brusquely to the side, lining up plates for service with brisk efficiency. "Spit it out then, I'm busy here."

Remy swiped a dollop of creme fraiche, licking it off her finger. "The haunting, Kari. It's back."

"Yes, I know, it's troubling." Kari hustled them towards the exit. "I've got beef wellingtons resting and a hot duck confit coming up. Do we have to discuss this right now?"

"Yes! It's just like last year," Remy exclaimed. "I thought we had moved past all this."

"We thought the shamans with their clearings and blessings and ceremony-ing had chased off the ghosts last year," Seth seconded. "But we were wrong."

Kari paused her chopping to meet Remy's eyes. "I agree the supernatural forces had not fully departed. The blessings the shaman performed last winter only restored balance temporarily."

Seth ran a hand through his hair anxiously. "If it's happening again, we need answers. My father..." His voice trailed off.

"It's been a year since your father passed, hasn't it?" Kari asked briskly.

Seth nodded. "Right before Christmas. And that's when the activity started up here at the resort. You don't think..."

"It could be his spirit?" Remy finished his sentence.

The three stood in contemplative silence until Kari spoke. "If it is your father, a seance may help us communicate with him and understand his unrest."

Remy and Seth exchanged uneasy glances.

"I know communing with the dead is frightening," Kari said. "But we must find the source of this disruption if the resort is to find peace."

Seth squared his shoulders. "You're right. We'll hold a seance tonight in my father's office."

Kari shook her head firmly at Seth. "Not tonight, can't you see I'm busy running a tight ship here?" She gestured at the controlled chaos of the kitchen, then continued "Besides, we need Destiny, Carson, her cat, and your dog."

"What's Destiny's cat got to do with this?" Seth asked, furrowing his brow.

Kari's eyes took on a mystical glint. "It has to do with our holiday theme of the year: serendipity. All the players must be present for the universe's plan to unfold."

Seth and Remy exchanged puzzled looks. But they had long ago learned to trust Kari's uncanny instincts.

"Very well," Seth conceded. "We'll arrange the seance for tomorrow then. Will you invite Destiny and Carson? Tell them they are required to attend."

Kari inclined her head in agreement, already turning back to expedite a tray of expertly seared scallops.

DESTINY CURLED up on the sofa, sipping her morning coffee as Velvet purred contentedly in her lap. Sunlight streamed through the windows of her cozy living room, glinting off the glittering ornaments on the Christmas tree. Despite the cheery decor, a pang of regret flickered through Destiny as she recalled the disastrous dinner last night.

She cringed at the thought of fleeing the resort after Carson laughed at her silly suspicions about his “Satan” nickname. She cringed even more thinking how she had sneaked through his coat like a ridiculous spy.

Destiny sighed, scratching Velvet behind her ears. "Oh, I really made a mess of things, didn't I?"

The cat blinked up at her with huge blue and green eyes, letting out a little mew in agreement

Just then, Destiny's phone buzzed with an incoming text.

"Seth thinks his dad's ghost is haunting the hotel and wants to do a seance. Pre-seance meeting in Remy's office at 11 am. Be there or be square."

She glanced at the clock. It was nearly 10 already. Downing the last of her coffee, Destiny hurried to get ready.

REMY USHERED the group into her office cluttered with an eclectic array of Christmas decorations and props. Seth and Remy took a seat in the lounger in the corner, his dog Benson curled up dutifully at his feet. Kari strode in confidently, with Destiny, and Carson following behind.

Once settled, Destiny set her bubble backpack on the floor and unzipped it to let Velvet out. Benson's tail wagged excitedly as he caught sight of the cat emerging from the backpack. He bounded over, nose twitching as he sniffed eagerly at the newcomer. Velvet eyed the exuberant dog warily, fur bristling as she backed up a few steps.

"Down boy," Seth called out gently. But Benson was transfixed by this new furry friend. He leaned in closer, tongue lolling in a happy grin and attempting to lick Velvet's face.

In a flash, Velvet lashed out with her paw, landing a light but firm whack right on Benson's nose, startling him enough to make him retreat behind Seth's legs.

"I see they're getting acquainted," Remy chuckled, watching the interaction unfold. Carson bit back a laugh while Destiny scooped up Velvet protectively.

"Don't mind him, Affenpinschers are just a bit overly friendly," Seth assured, giving Benson's head an affectionate rub. The dog whined, tail between his legs as he eyed Velvet from a safer distance. Destiny smoothed down her cat's fur, whispering soothingly.

Seth cleared his throat, calling the group to attention. "Thank you all for coming. I know things have been strange around here lately." He paused, clasping his hands together.

"As some of you may have guessed, we believe this resort is experiencing... a haunting." Seth's voice was solemn, his expression grim. "The timing is no coincidence. The bizarre activity started around Christmas last year. The same time my father, Lance Conley, passed away."

He exhaled slowly, shoulders slumping. "My father built this place. It was his pride and joy. Losing him was a tremendous blow, but the fact is in the year leading up to his death, my father's behavior had been growing increasingly erratic, and obsessive, almost like he was a different person. I thought it was just his health, but....." Seth's voice trailed off as emotions swept over him. Benson nuzzled his hand supportively.

"Anyway, we need to get to the bottom of whatever is haunting this resort before things escalate further. Remy and I thought, given the timing and circumstance of it all, there was a chance my father's death was somehow related to it. And Kari has suggested we can do a seance to try to contact him. Will you help us?"

Carson leaned forward in his seat. "Of course, we'll help, Seth."

"Velvet and I will help with whatever we can," Destiny added sincerely. "Just tell us what to do."

"Alright folks," Kari took charge of the room. "Tonight we're going to hold a séance and try to contact Lance Conley's spirit. But first, a few ground rules."

Kari looked around the room, making eye contact with each person gathered. "Before we begin the séance tonight, I want you all to understand that there are no coincidences," she stated. "Each of you was brought here for a reason. Destiny, you grew up here but left to find your own path. Yet for some reason, you returned to Christmas Hills now, of all times." Destiny nodded in agreement.

"And Carson-" Kari continued, "Your malfunctioning phone led you right where you needed to be: Destiny's gift shop, the hotel your old colleague Remy now manages, Pat's general store where he gave you the strange gift of a planchette, and the fact your room is right across from room 1302, the latest addition to our short list of haunting sites."

Carson blinked, taking this in. He was not aware of strange things occurring in the room across from his. The series of events did seem oddly serendipitous in hindsight.

"Furthermore," Kari went on, "we have two very special animals with us." She smiled down at Velvet, whose dichromatic eyes stared back knowingly. "Cats born with two different colored eyes are believed to have one paw in the physical world and the other more firmly rooted in the spiritual realm than normal cats."

Velvet purred in response. Kari then nodded towards Benson. "And this little guy, we already know from experience, has a nose for deceit. He'll alert us to any ill intent." Benson wagged his tail proudly.

"My point is, whether by destiny or sheer luck, we have exactly who and what we need for tonight's ritual. Magic relies a great deal on serendipity - being receptive to the signs the universe provides. Trust in the signs that brought you here, and in each other, this is the key to the séance tonight."

Kari's motivational words stirred courage and purpose within the group. They exchanged resolute glances, ready to embrace whatever the night held.

Kari continued. "So tonight, we'll use the planchette on an Ouija board to contact old Mr. Conley. I'll secure a board before tonight, along with candles and other necessary items." She shot Carson a pointed look. "Don't lose yours before then."

"Wouldn't dream of it," Carson replied.

Kari smirked. "Good. Now a séance requires open minds and patience. I'll guide the ritual, but everyone must contribute positive energy and concentration." Her eyes narrowed, tone growing serious. "And under no circumstances will anyone break the circle once we've begun. That would unleash unpredictable forces."

Seth shifted uncomfortably at this warning while Destiny bit her lip nervously.

"Hey, don't look so gloomy! I'll be doing most of the hard work but you guys are also participants." Kari's expression softened into a sly grin. "Don't look so gloomy, I promise plenty of snacks afterward."

This elicited a few relieved chuckles. Kari rubbed her hands together, gearing up to explain more. But first, she paused, meeting each person's gaze. "Any questions before I go over the ritual process?"

Destiny raised her hand tentatively. "Will it...hurt?"

Kari laughed. "Only if you get possessed by a spirit!" Then her tone gentled. "No, you'll be perfectly safe. I'll make certain of it."

Remy looked over at Kari. "Where do you think would be the best place to hold the séance tonight?" she asked.

Kari pursed her lips, considering the question. "Typically, it's most effective to conduct a séance in an area where there has been significant paranormal activity," she replied after a moment. "In this case, that would be my kitchen. However..." She trailed off, frowning slightly.

"The kitchen is constantly in use to prepare meals for the guests," Remy finished Kari's thought. "It wouldn't be very practical to hold a séance there."

Kari nodded in agreement. "Yes, exactly. A more private place would be much more preferable."

"Why don't we start in room 1302, the freezing room across from Carson's?" Seth suggested as he tapped his chin thoughtfully.

Carson's eyebrows shot up in surprise, but Kari stood up decisively. "Perfect. Room 1302 it is then. We'll gather there at nine o'clock to begin the séance." And with that, she walked out the door without a backward glance.

DESTINY STRODE out of Remy's office with Velvet bouncing slightly inside the bubble backpack. Carson found himself going after her once again, this time he had no difficulty catching up to her.

"Destiny, got a minute?" She stopped and spun around to face him.

"Hey," he began tentatively. "How's your morning going? Besides plotting séances and ghost huntings?"

A pause, then, "Fine." Her tone was guarded.

"Good, good." Carson ran a hand through his hair, grasping for the right words. "Listen, about last night..."

"I'm really sorry," Destiny interjected. "I shouldn't have gone through your things. That was wrong of me."

"I appreciate the apology," Carson said quickly. "And I'm sorry too, for laughing. I shouldn't have dismissed your concerns like that."

Destiny exhaled in relief. "Thanks. I guess everything happening around here just put me on edge. But I want to start fresh if you do."

"Absolutely. No more suspicions, no more spying. Deal?" Carson grinned.

"Deal." He thought he heard a hint of a smile in her voice.

An awkward pause stretched between them before Carson broke the silence. "For what it's worth, I was serious about wanting to help you promote your culinary talents. You're incredibly gifted in the kitchen."

Destiny shook her head dismissively. "You're too kind, but I'm really not that great of a chef."

"Are you kidding me?" Carson exclaimed. "Dinner two nights ago was of such high caliber that it could have been served in a fine dining establishment. And trust me, I'm very familiar with fine dining."

"I don't know..." Destiny trailed off uncertainly.

"Hey, you've been helping me to regain my joy of Christmas," Carson pointed out gently. "Let me return the favor. At least think about it?"

Destiny hesitated before nodding. "Alright, I'll consider it. But first, let's get through this séance in one piece," she said wryly.

Carson chuckled. "Deal. See you later then?"

She smiled and felt the tension dissipating from her body. The prospect of the séance no longer appeared as intimidating as it had just a short while earlier.

DESTINY SHIVERED as she stepped into the frigid room 1302, rubbing her mitten-clad hands together for warmth. Carson was already there, hovering near the door.

"Sorry I'm a few minutes late, I was um... you know what they say about herding cats," Destiny said as she set the bubble backpack on the floor to let Velvet out.

"No worries, I was just early since I literally live just a couple of steps away," Carson attempted a lighthearted response but his smile didn't reach his eyes.

The old floorboards creaked underfoot as Seth and Remy entered, followed by the little dog Benson, who was wearing a red bowtie. Velvet eyed Benson warily, the memory of the dog's over-enthusiasm still fresh on her mind.

Kari had arranged candles around a round wooden table draped in purple velvet. The flickering flames cast dancing shadows on the peeling floral wallpaper, faded from age and neglect. Destiny counted seven chairs and seven candles, one for each human and animal. On the table sat a large rectangular board with spaced-out letters and numbers arranged in three arcing rows.

"Shall we begin?" Kari asked as she handed a cushion each to Destiny and Seth, meant for Velvet and Benson.

Clasping hands around the table, the group sat in tense silence. The candles guttered in a sudden draft, and Destiny's breath caught. She met Carson's eyes, seeing her own trepidation mirrored.

Kari surveyed the faces of the seance participants - immediately to her right sat Velvet in a cushion perched on a chair. Next to Velvet sat Destiny and Carson side-by-side. To her left, Seth and Remy watched her expectantly, with Benson snoozing in a dog bed on a chair between them.

"Before we begin, I want to remind you all of what we discussed earlier today," Kari said, her voice low but firm. "When contacting the spirit realm, it is vital that we maintain positive intentions and not allow fear to take hold. The candles on this table have been spelled, they act as an indicator of your resolve. If you see your candle flickering or going dim, it's a sign you need to strengthen your intent."

She paused, meeting each person's gaze in turn. "Remember - we all have to keep our holds on the planchette. No matter what occurs, we must not let go and have at least one hand each on the planchette, until I've performed the closing ceremony."

"What about Velvet and Benson?" Destiny asked.

"They don't need to use their paws, they're already present one hundred percent just by being here."

Kari picked up the metal planchette that Carson had received from Pat and murmured words in an unknown language that sounded ancient and melodic.

"Now, let us start," she said, placing the planchette on the board and her fingers on the planchette. The others followed suit, placing their fingers nervously until they formed an unbroken chain.

Kari closed her eyes. "Spirit who resides in this place, we ask that you make yourself known," Kari intoned. "We mean you no harm - only seek to understand you and provide a resolution. Give us a sign of your presence."

A tense silence followed. The very air seemed charged with anticipation. Then slowly, almost imperceptibly, the planchette began to slide across the board.

The planchette glided haltingly across the board. It paused over the letter C, then moved to the O. Kari's eyes widened as it traced out the letters N, L, E, and Y.

"Conley," Remy breathed out in surprise. "It's spelling your family name, Seth."

Seth stared at the board, his face pale. Benson let out a soft whine.

"Spirit, we thank you for identifying yourself," Kari said evenly. "Might we ask, which Conley family member are you?"

Again the planchette crawled into motion, more smoothly now that the connection was established. It arced to the C, then O, N, L, E, and Y.

"It's not understanding us," Seth fretted.

"Don't get frustrated, stay focused," Kari murmured.

"Spirit, can you tell us why you are still here?" Kari asked gently but firmly.

The planchette circled the board aimlessly, then centered over the word NO.

"Are you unable to tell us?" Kari clarified.

The planchette again circled the board aimlessly.

Kari's brows furrowed and tried a different approach. "Are you trapped here against your will?"

The séance participants waited with bated breath, but no response came from the planchette. Instead, a strange cracking sound filled the room. Destiny's gaze shot to the radiator in the corner, watching in disbelief as icicles began forming rapidly across its grated front.

"What's happening?" Remy gasped.

"Spirit, what is it that you want from us?" Kari asked again.

Velvet's ears perked up as she stared intently at the ceiling, and started to chirp.

"What is it, kitty?" Destiny asked, momentarily distracted by the strange sound her cat was making. She followed the Velvet's gaze but the ceiling offered no clues.

Kari's eyes narrowed, her focus torn between the planchette and the cat's puzzling behavior. "Destiny, does she do this often?"

"Only when she's spotted something to pounce on, like a bug or a moth that I can't see," Destiny explained with a mystified shrug.

Velvet's chirping grew steadily louder when Benson suddenly let out a ferocious growl. All eyes turned as the small dog stood up in his dog bed and started barking fiercely at the same spot on the ceiling.

"Seth, look.... " Remy shuddered as she saw a thin sheath of frost creeping over Benson's dog bed, encrusting the cushion in delicate fernlike crystals.

"Are you trying to harm Benson?" Seth demanded, instinctively freeing up one hand to pull the affenpinscher closer. The planchette lay motionless.

"Whatever presence is here does not seem interested in communicating directly," Kari said grimly. "Yet its displeasure is made clear." She began chanting in her native tongue, no doubt reciting protective incantations.

"We need to end this now!" Remy cried. As if in answer, all the candles started dancing wildly as if an unnatural wind howled through the room.

"We need to refocus and close this session," Kari declared, "I'm going to need all of your energy and intent to do this properly."

Kari's voice rang out clear and strong as she chanted the closing incantations for the séance. Her eyes were closed in deep concentration, one hand gripping the planchette while the other made intricate gestures over the board.

With a final lyrical phrase, the flickering candles steadied and Kari lifted the planchette off the board to set it aside. A collective exhale sounded around the table as the connection was severed. Kari opened her eyes, her face pale but resolute.

"It is done. The doorway is closed."

The others sat in shaken silence. Benson whimpered and burrowed into Seth's lap. Destiny reached a comforting hand down to stroke Velvet, who was alert but no longer fixated on the ceiling.

Remy glanced over at the radiator and gasped. "The ice - it's gone!"

They followed her gaze. Indeed, no trace of the sinister frost remained. Yet the room's temperature was still frigid enough to see their own breaths.

Kari rose and began gathering the candles. "We have much to discuss about what occurred here tonight," she said gravely. "But first, I recommend we move somewhere warmer and have some hot drinks to revive ourselves."

Chapter Eight

Remy's office, with its crackling fireplace and plush furnishings, offered a much-needed comforting respite from the bone-chilling séance in room 1302. As the weary group retreated here to warm up, Kari ordered a lavish late-night feast from the kitchen to revive their spirits. Soon, steaming mugs of creamy hot chocolate arrived, topped with mounds of whipped cream and shavings of dark chocolate. Hearty bowls of French onion soup emerged, the broth rich and savory, with melted Gruyère cheese stretching in gooey strings across toasted bread. Mini beef wellingtons followed, the puff pastry golden and flaky, enveloping tender filet mignon and savory duxelles. For a sweet finish, flourless chocolate cakes landed on the table, dark, dense, and decadent.

"This hot chocolate is pure magic - I can already feel my bones thawing out," Carson said, closing his eyes as he took a long sip from the steaming mug.

"And this French onion soup is melting all my troubles away. Kari, you're a mind reader with this menu." Destiny joined in agreement from the plush chair by the fireplace, grateful for the feast Kari had arranged.

Kari smiled. "After that séance, we all needed some real food and warmth."

The friends ate in contented silence for a few moments before Remy spoke up. "So... any thoughts on what happened in room 1302 tonight?"

Seth shook his head, looking troubled. "All I know is we kept hearing my last name, 'Conley.' Over and over."

"And the way those icicles just... grew... from the radiators," Remy added with a shiver. "That was downright creepy."

Kari nodded. "I've never seen anything like it. And when the ice crystals started forming around Benson..."

Benson whined softly at the mention of his name, and Velvet nuzzled him reassuringly. They seemed to have bonded over the ordeal and were now enjoying their portions from Kari's kitchen.

"It's clear something supernatural is going on here," Remy said. "But the séance didn't give us any real answers about the nature of this haunting."

Destiny set down her cake fork, turning to Seth. "Did your father ever mention having any regrets or unfinished business when he was alive? Anything that might make his spirit linger?"

Seth shook his head, his expression darkening. "My father was in a downward spiral the last year of his life. It was so gradual at first. But then the obsession set in. He became consumed with something, but I don't know what."

Kari tapped her chin thoughtfully. "Was there anything in his life around that time? Anything that might have triggered his change in behavior?"

Seth pondered for a moment. "Now that you mention it, there was a hotel guest death about two years ago. It happened on Christmas Eve." His eyes widened slightly as realization dawned. "Come to think of it, Father started acting strange not long after that. At first, it was subtle - he spent more time holed up in his office going through old records and journals. But within a few months, the obsession had taken hold."

Destiny leaned forward, intrigued. "What happened to the guest who died?"

"It was an older gentleman," Seth replied. "He had some chronic health issues. Father said he passed away peacefully in his sleep from natural causes."

Carson scratched his chin. "A natural death of a random hotel guest doesn't sound like something to obsess over."

"What about the icicles and frost on the radiator and Benson's dog bed? I couldn't help but notice how uneasy Benson seemed during the session." Sensing the conversation was at a dead end, Destiny attempted to bring some other angles back into the discussion about the séance.

She looked thoughtful for a moment before adding, "What if Seth's father is the one haunting this place? From what you've said about his obsession and declining mental state, it sounds like he had unfinished business when he died. And with it being so close to Christmas again, the time when he passed, maybe his spirit is restless."

Seth sighed. "I hate to think of my father's ghost trapped here, unable to move on. Especially if he's lonely or confused, although that would maybe explain Benson's behavior."

Noticing Carson's puzzled expression, Seth continued, "Benson was my father's dog. They were extremely close. If my father's ghost is feeling lonely, he might be reaching out to Benson for companionship, but Benson is just a little pup and not used to ghosts, are you Benson?" Seth picked the little dog up to sit him in his lap as Benson wagged his tail.

"So what can we do about this, Kari? Do you have any ideas for pacifying the spirit or spirits haunting the hotel?" Remy leaned forward in her chair.

Kari nodded thoughtfully. "Well, the first step is always figuring out what the ghost wants. What's keeping them tethered here instead of passing on? There must be some unfinished business or deep regret anchoring them to this plane."

"I'm not sacrificing little Benson here, no way," Seth responded firmly.

She glanced over at Seth. "I know your first thought went to protecting little Benson here." She gave the dog a gentle pat on the head. "But don't worry, one's love for a pet is rarely enough to cause a haunting. If we are talking about your father's ghost, we need to look into his obsession more."

Seth let out a small sigh of relief as he continued stroking Benson's fur. "That's good to know."

Kari turned her gaze to Seth, her expression serious. "I know this is difficult, but you need to search your memories for any clue about what was consuming your father in those final months. Any detail could help us understand why he can't move on."

Seth looked around at the group gathered in Remy's office, his expression conflicted. "I just don't know," he admitted with a frustrated sigh. "Ever since my father passed, I've wondered about the changes in his personality that last year. But I could never figure out what happened to make him become so obsessed and erratic."

Remy reached over and gave Seth's hand a supportive squeeze. "We want to help you get to the bottom of this," she said gently. "If you'll let us, that is."

Seth hesitated, glancing down at his hands. "Part of me wants answers," he said slowly. "But another part worries about what we might uncover. My father had such a strong public image. I'm afraid of finding out he was...losing his mind at the end."

"We understand your reservations," Carson said. "But keeping this bottled up won't bring you peace. Let us help you uncover the truth."

Kari nodded. "Spirits trapped between realms rarely find rest on their own. We need to get to the bottom of your father's obsession and hopefully help his soul pass on."

Destiny chimed in softly. "Please let us help, Seth. Whatever we discover, it will stay between us."

Seth looked around at the sincere faces surrounding him. Finally, he nodded. "Alright. If you all are willing, not only would I accept, but greatly appreciate your help. I want to find out what consumed my father that last year and see if we can put his spirit to rest."

"It's decided then," Remy said. "We'll start investigating. And we'll keep an eye out for any more strange occurrences around the hotel that could be his ghost trying to communicate."

"But please, we need to keep the details of this investigation between us, and us only. Do I have your word?"

"We promise this stays between us, no matter what we uncover," Carson added. "You have our word."

"Thank you, all of you," he said, relieved. "I can't thank you enough. Why don't we all go to my office to have a round of drinks on me and seal the deal? Let me show my appreciation."

SETH LED the small group of friends down the hallway towards the warm glow and chatter emanating from the resort's lively lounge. Carson let out a chuckle when he realized Seth's "office" turned out to be the hotel bar.

As they entered, the bartender glanced up from polishing glasses. Taking in their pale, shaken expressions, he raised an eyebrow.

"Rough night, boss? You all look like you've seen a ghost."

Seth gave a wry chuckle at the inadvertently accurate quip. "Something like that. Everyone, meet Jaime Luis Hernandez, bartender extraordinaire."

"I have just the thing you need, nothing like homemade eggnog to warm you up and we just made a fresh batch today."

"Sounds excellent. We'll take a round."

Jaime's eyes twinkled knowingly as he lined up a row of glass mugs and ladled out generous portions of his secret-recipe eggnog, then topped them with whipped cream and cinnamon.

The group gathered at the end of the bar, gratefully accepting the festive drinks. As Jaime slid the last eggnog down the bar, he held up his mug.

"To our secret pact," Seth announced, meeting each person's eyes sincerely.

"Here here," Kari chimed in as everyone clinked glasses and downed the spiced eggnog and burning whiskey.

Seth set his empty mug down firmly. "It's official now. We're in this together. Jaime, pour the usual for me and a round of whatever these guys want as well."

"I'll drink to that," Jaime chuckled, topping off their mugs with more of the creamy libation.

A few rounds of Jaime's potent drinks later, everyone's inhibition loosened.

"So what got you all so spooked before you came here?" Jaime asked.

"We held a séance earlier trying to channel my father's spirit."

The group froze, exchanging startled glances. Remy cleared her throat pointedly. "Seth, dear, remember what we discussed about discretion?"

But Seth waved away her concern tipsily. "It's fine, it's just Jaime. He and my father were thick as thieves. Weren't you, Jaime?"

Jaime blinked in surprise but recovered quickly. "Oh yes, Mr. Conley and I always got on well. He came down to the bar and mingled with the guests often, ever the gracious host." A nostalgic smile crossed the bartender's face.

Seeing an opening, Seth leaned forward eagerly across the bar. "Since you see guests come and go all the time, maybe you can help shed some light on what happened a couple of years ago. There was a guest here a couple of years ago, older gentleman, stayed at the hotel during the holidays and unfortunately, it happened to be his time and he passed away in his room."

"Hmm, two years back around Christmas..." Jaime murmured, brow furrowing as he tried to recall the details. Then he snapped his fingers. "Oh yes, I remember now! It was Mr. McDowell, wasn't it? Richard McDowell if I'm not mistaken."

Destiny and Carson exchanged startled glances.

"Wow! You must have an amazing memory to be able to recall the name of a single guest after two years!" Carson remarked.

"Not really, it's more of an occupational hazard and a curse. Also, we had a nickname for him, so I'm helped by mnemonics."

"What was his nickname?" Destiny felt curious.

"Oh, just something silly." Jaime tried to brush her question off, then leaned in and said in a lower voice, "I don't want you to think we nickname guests behind their backs all the time."

"Well, what do you remember about this guy that you can tell us?" Carson asked.

Jaime leaned back against the counter, the dim light of the bar casting a warm glow over his face. "Ah, Richard McDowell," he mused. "He was a grumpy one, alright. Always had something to complain about. And at the end of his rants, he'd take a deep puff from his asthma inhaler like it was some sort of exclamation point. Granted, he wasn't like the other guests who had wanted to be here for the holidays. Richard's car broke down in a blizzard while driving through this area. With no mechanics working during the holidays he was stuck here, he'd had no choice but to book a room. I guess that made him even grumpier."

Destiny's gaze sharpened with interest. "Hmm, sounds familiar," she gave Carson a side glance. "Did he interact much with other guests?"

"Not really," Jaime shrugged. "He preferred the solitude of his room after a couple of nightcaps here at the bar. Always the same drink, too—Lagavulin 16, neat."

Carson's lips twitched in amusement. "Sounds like he had good taste in Scotch at least."

Jaime chuckled, nodding. "Except for this one evening when your father joined him, Seth." He nodded toward Seth, who was listening intently. "They got into quite the holiday spirit that night—drank more eggnog than anyone could count."

"And what were they talking about?" Seth asked, leaning closer.

"Mostly about being rich and all the paranoia that comes with it, if I remember correctly. You know, hiding assets, not trusting banks or people, not trusting the hotel safe, that sort of thing."

Seth furrowed his brow thoughtfully but said nothing.

Remy tilted her head curiously. "Do you know how Mr. McDowell died exactly?"

Jaime wiped down a glass absentmindedly before answering. "No details really — it was all very uneventful from what I heard. Happened a day or so after Christmas. They said he died in his sleep or something along those lines."

Seth drained the last of his eggnog, the warmth spreading through his chest like a soothing balm. He glanced at Remy, who had been a pillar of strength throughout the night's unsettling revelations. "I think it's time we head back," he murmured, offering her a tired but grateful smile.

"Agreed," Remy replied, patting his hand gently. "You two," she gestured to Carson and Destiny, "don't stay up too late plotting your culinary takeover." Her teasing tone belied the exhaustion in her eyes as they stood to leave.

Once Seth and Remy had departed, the atmosphere around the bar shifted to a more intimate setting. The remaining trio found themselves in a contemplative silence before Carson broke it.

"Destiny," he began earnestly, leaning across the bar towards her. "About the website and filming... I wasn't just talking to make conversation. I really believe in your talent."

Destiny fiddled with her mug, her cheeks flushed not from the eggnog but from the swell of imposter syndrome bubbling within her. "I... don't know," she hesitated. "I'm not sure I'm ready for that kind of exposure."

Kari had been listening quietly, nursing a glass of wine. She chimed in smoothly, "Nonsense. You're more than ready."

Carson nodded at Kari's affirmation and jumped on the opportunity. "Exactly. And what better place to showcase your skills than in the hotel's kitchen? Kari, do you think we could shoot some footage there?"

Kari set down her wine glass and considered their request. A moment passed before she answered with a decisive nod. "There's usually a lull between breakfast and lunch service every day. We can make that work."

"Great! Can we start tomorrow?" Carson's eyes gleamed with excitement.

Kari shrugged casually. "Fine by me."

Destiny bit her lip. She met Kari's encouraging gaze and found herself bolstered by it. With a tentative nod, she said, "Okay, let's do it."

Carson beamed at her response. "Think about what you want to make and bring those ideas to breakfast tomorrow morning. We'll go over everything then."

"You'll have access to all my tools and whatever you need from the pantry, but remember to bring your main ingredients," Kari reminded Destiny as she prepared to leave.

Destiny finally allowed herself to feel a flicker of excitement at the prospect of sharing her culinary creations with the world —or at least with Carson's camera for now.

"Thanks, Kari." Destiny smiled broadly for the first time that evening.

Kari returned the smile with a wink, then disappeared into the quiet halls of the resort.

Alone now with Carson, Destiny stood up from her stool, invigorated by their plans but also aware of how much preparation lay ahead of her.

"I'd better head home and do my homework then," she said with newfound determination in her voice.

Carson watched her stand with admiration shining in his eyes. "Goodnight, Destiny," he called after her retreating figure.

"Goodnight, Carson!" Destiny called back over her shoulder as she exited the bar, energized by the plans to film her culinary skills the next day.

Chapter Nine

Destiny woke up before dawn, anticipation stirring in her belly for the day ahead. She dressed warmly against the winter chill and headed to the Christmas Hills Farmer's Market, hoping to find the freshest ingredients for the lima bean and sweet pepper gratin she planned to prepare.

Strings of twinkling lights adorned the market's wooden rafters, casting a festive glow over the bustling stalls. Vendors called out cheerful greetings, their booths overflowing with seasonal produce. Destiny breathed deeply, inhaling the mingling scents of cinnamon, cloves, and pine.

At the bean stall, she hand-selected plump, velvety lima beans, imagining how their creamy texture would pair with the smoky bacon and melted cheese. Next, she chose vibrant red and yellow bell peppers, farm-fresh eggs, and a wedge of aged Parmigiano-Reggiano. The cheese seller wrapped it in muslin, handing it to Destiny with a wink and a sample taste that oozed nutty, complex flavors.

With her ingredients secured in a wicker basket, Destiny got in her jeep. She realized, for the first time in years, she felt a glimmer of festive joy.

On the drive to the Christmas Hills Hotel, she passed by the spot where Carson's rental car had spun out and hit a tree just days before. She made a mental note to ask him if he ever got that situation sorted out.

Once parked, she hurried towards the entrance of the Christmas Hills Hotel, the sight of Carson waiting for her arrival in the hotel lobby sending a smile to her face. She picked up her pace, excited to greet him. But just as she crossed the driveway, the clip-clop of approaching hooves made her turn. A magnificent Clydesdale carriage rounded the Rotonda, piloted by two top-hatted drivers. Destiny jumped back just in time to avoid a collision, but the basket of precious ingredients tumbled from her grip, scattering eggs and vegetables across the snowy driveway.

"Oh no!" Destiny cried out, so horrified at the mess of wasted food that she didn't notice her jeans were smeared with snow and sludge. She crouched down, attempting to gather up the ruined groceries.

The drivers of the carriage hopped out of the carriage to check on Destiny. The brawny one asked if she was hurt while the other one with the stature of a racing jockey, helped gather the spilled groceries.

Carson rushed over, concern evident in his furrowed brows. "Are you okay?"

Destiny nodded.

"Hi, I'm Freud," the jockey introduced himself.

"And I'm Jung," said the brawny one.

"I don't think I've ever met anyone actually named Freud," Carson commented with an amused grin.

They both laughed. "Our parents were psychologists," Jung explained. "Ironic they didn't consider the psychological impact of peculiar names on their kids."

After ensuring Destiny was uninjured, Jung said, "I'm glad you're alright. Don't want a repeat of what happened to Vincent two years ago."

"The guy at the front desk?" Carson asked. "What happened?"

"Similar carriage mishap on Christmas Eve," said Freud. "But Vincent wasn't as graceful as Destiny here. Ended up with a broken arm."

Jung added, "Craziest Christmas we've ever had. Blizzard rolled in, stressed out the horses. Total chaos at the hotel dinner service. We had to help the staff haul in palettes of extra dishes when a whole kitchen shelf fell down."

Freud chimed in, "And the boiler crises later that day. Had to wake up ol' Pat Ferguson at the general store too, to bring space heaters for the guests at 2 am!"

The brothers helped Destiny collect the rest of her spilled basket before continuing on their carriage ride.

Dismay sank in as she realized there was no way she could salvage enough for the elaborate gratin. Carson squeezed her shoulder reassuringly.

"Don't worry, we'll figure something out," he said. "Maybe Kari has extras in the kitchen?"

As THEY FINISHED up their delicious breakfast at the resort and dabbed their mouths with linen napkins, Kari emerged from the kitchen, her chef's whites crisp and pristine.

"Good morning!" she greeted them brightly. "I hope you both enjoyed the meal."

Destiny's eyes lit up at the sight of the statuesque chef. "It was phenomenal as always, Kari. You've really outdone yourself!"

Destiny and Carson had enjoyed a mouthwatering spread - fluffy pancakes drizzled with maple syrup, crispy bacon, scrambled eggs sprinkled with chives, and freshly squeezed orange juice. It was so delicious that she had almost completely forgotten about her mishap with the carriage earlier.

Kari waved her hand modestly. "Oh please, it's just a little something I whipped up. Now come, let me give you a tour of my kitchen before the lunch rush chaos begins!"

"Kari, I... unfortunately, spilled all the ingredients I brought this morning. So we probably have to postpone the shooting plan to another time." Destiny said sheepishly.

"What were you going to make?"

"Baby lima bean and sweet pepper gratin," Destiny replied, her cheeks flushing pink with embarrassment.

Kari patted her gently on the back and said, "Don't you worry, I've got your back. You'll be whipping up that gratin in no time." Destiny felt a wave of relief wash over her. Of course, Kari would understand - she was not just an incredible chef, but her kind and gracious mentor.

As they made their way into the bustling kitchen, Destiny inhaled the intoxicating scents of simmering sauces and sizzling meats. Christmas music played softly in the background as the staff hustled about, prepping for the lunch service. She took in the sight of the gleaming stainless steel, the racks of gleaming copper pots, and the towers of perfectly arranged ingredients. This was Destiny's happy place. With Kari's help, they quickly gathered the necessary ingredients for the gratin.

Carson unpacked his camera equipment - just a simple DSLR camera, a tripod, and his iPhone. He wanted to keep the shoot relaxed and informal to help Destiny feel comfortable.

"Don't worry, we'll just have some fun with this," Carson said, giving Destiny an encouraging smile.

He adjusted the camera settings, angling it towards the middle island where Destiny would be cooking, framing the shot to capture the beautiful copper pots hanging in the background.

"Are you ready?" he asked.

Destiny nodded, determination setting into her delicate features.

Carson hit record as Destiny began explaining the dish, her voice clear but tentative. Occasionally he would interject an insightful question, helping Destiny open up on camera. He filmed her as she prepped the ingredients for the lima bean gratin. She was nervous but also excited for this opportunity. As she layered the tender lima beans and colorful peppers into the dish, Destiny felt a familiar creative energy take hold. She was back in her element, doing what she loved most.

As the dish baked, filling the kitchen with irresistible aromas of garlic, thyme, and melty Gruyère cheese, Carson switched to taking still shots on his DSLR. He snapped photos of Destiny drizzling olive oil, sprinkling herbs, and peeking into the oven. Destiny started to relax, laughing and hamming it up for the camera. When the gratin emerged, golden and bubbling, Carson captured Destiny's proud smile. "That looks amazing!" Carson said. He could see her confidence growing as they reviewed the footage together. This was only the beginning, he thought.

KARI WATCHED INTENTLY as Destiny expertly assembled the gratin. She was struck by just how skilled her young protégé had become. Where once there was hesitance, now there was confidence and flair.

After the filming wrapped up, Kari pulled Destiny aside. "You've really come into your own," she said warmly. "Your skills have reached an entirely new level."

Destiny blushed at the praise. "You really think so?"

"I know so," Kari replied. She leaned in conspiratorially. "In fact, I believe your talents extend beyond the culinary arts. Your abilities hint at... greater gifts."

Destiny's eyes widened. "You don't mean..."

"Oh, but I do," said Kari with a knowing smile. "Cooking and magic have more in common than you realize, Destiny. I believe you have the potential for both."

Destiny was shocked. Is Kari saying what she thinks she's saying?

"I... I don't know what to say," Destiny stammered.

"You needn't say anything just yet," Kari reassured her. "I know this is a lot to take in. But I've been searching for the right apprentice to share my knowledge with. And I believe I've found her in you."

Excitement bloomed in Destiny's chest, but uncertainty still lingered. "Are you sure about me?" she asked hesitantly. "I mean, most of the time I'm just a bumbling..."

"You have a rare gift, Destiny," Kari said firmly. "With time and training, you will see it too. For now, trust me. Will you accept an apprenticeship under my guidance? You don't have to answer now, take your time, think about it, mull it over."

Destiny could hardly believe this was happening. To learn magic and cooking from the legendary Kari Magnusson...it was a dream come true.

"Yes!" she exclaimed. "I accept!"

Kari grinned, her blue eyes twinkling. "Excellent. We will start, as soon as the holidays are over. For now, go impress some guests with your superb gratin."

Chapter Ten

As Destiny got rid of the remaining evidence of their invasion of Kari's kitchen and finished cleaning up, Carson's phone vibrated against the stainless steel countertop. He glanced at the screen, finding Remy's name illuminated against a backdrop of unread messages.

"Remy's asking if we've uncovered anything new," he said, turning to Destiny with an inquisitive tilt of his head.

Destiny wiped her hands on a towel, thoughtfully. "I think we need to dig deeper into what happened two years ago," she mused. "From Freud and Jung this morning, it sounded like that Christmas Eve was exceptionally chaotic. I wonder if the chaos played into the death of Richard McDowell or Seth's dad's obsession, or both."

Carson leaned against the counter, recalling fragments of conversations with Freud and Jung. Vincent's accident with the carriage, the epic blizzard that cut through the town, kitchen chaos, boiler problems, and Richard McDowell's death shortly after Christmas. The memories seemed like pieces of a puzzle if they could just manage to fit them together.

"The bar," he said. "Jaime might be more willing to talk openly when his boss isn't present."

"Good point. Besides, I wouldn't mind having some more of that delicious eggnog." Destiny winked

Nodding in agreement, Carson pocketed his phone and followed Destiny out of the kitchen. The resort's corridors echoed with the laughter and chatter of guests oblivious to the undercurrents that tugged at its foundations.

They found Jaime polishing glasses behind the bar, his hands moving with mechanical precision while his mouth curved into a lopsided smile at their approach.

"Hi Jaime," Carson greeted him. "We want to make sure you're not bored, or being burdened with too much eggnog."

Jaime laughed, "I appreciate that, very considerate of you. Your timing is perfect, I was just hoping someone would show up and help me get rid of the last bit of eggnog so we can make a new batch," he poured two generous portions and topped the mugs with a swirl of whipped cream and threw two sticks of cinnamon in.

Destiny took a sip of the eggnog through the cinnamon bark straw and felt the warmth of the whisky spread pleasantly over her body and instantly relaxed. "So, what would it take for you to tell us what Richard McDowell's nickname was?"

Jaime leaned in closer, his eyes darting around before he whispered, "Scrooge McDuck."

Carson burst out laughing, nearly falling off his barstool. Destiny pressed her lips together, trying not to join in, though she had to admit it was a fitting nickname.

"Honestly, Scrooge McDick would be more accurate," Jaime added with a smirk. "The guy was a real dick."

Just then, a cold gust of wind blew through the bar, making them all shiver. With a crash, a bottle toppled off the top shelf, shattering on the floor. The air was instantly filled with the aroma of expensive scotch.

"That... that was Richard's bottle. The one he had every night for a nightcap," Jaime stammered.

Destiny and Carson exchanged uneasy glances as Jaime stood pale-faced and trembling, staring at the broken bottle on the floor.

"I think we just got a message from our ghostly resident," Carson said in a low voice. "He clearly doesn't want us prying into Richard's story."

"Either that or Richard doesn't like his nickname," Jaime muttered.

Destiny nodded slowly. "Which probably means we're on the right track. Richard must have some connection to the haunting."

She reached over the bar to put a comforting hand on Jaime's shoulder. "Are you okay? I know that was unsettling."

Jaime took a shaky breath. "I'll be alright. But I don't think I can handle talking about Richard anymore right now."

"No problem, we understand," Carson said kindly. He pulled out his wallet. "Let me buy us a round of eggnogs to steady our nerves. I think we could all use one after that little spectacle."

Jaime gave him a grateful look and busied himself making three fresh mugs of eggnog. The familiar motions seemed to calm him, color returning to his cheeks. He downed his drink in one fell swoop and immediately poured himself another. Halfway through the second one, he seemed to have calmed down a bit.

"Are you feeling a little better?" Destiny checked in with him gently.

"I'm alright." Jaime looked down at his drink and frowned. "Remember when you were all here the other evening, and I mentioned the night when Richard and old Mr. Conley were getting drunk on eggnog at the bar?" Destiny nodded. "You know, there was something else. I didn't want to talk too much about old Mr. Conley in front of Seth, but, I think it's probably important and I should tell you two."

Carson looked over at Destiny and mouthed the words "Told you," elated at his intuition proving right that Jaime would open up more without Seth around.

"Sure, it's just between us," Destiny said gently. "Anything you can remember might help put these pieces together."

Jaime sighed, his eyes darting around the room despite it being empty except for the three of them. "That night, Mr. Conley kept supplying Richard with eggnog after eggnog. I figured he was just being hospitable, chatting with a guest, you know? But Richard got really drunk. I heard him mention something about hiding his money in a way no one could ever find."

Carson and Destiny exchanged a look. This sounded promising.

"Did he say anything else?" Carson asked. "Anything about where he hid it?"

Jaime shook his head. "Not that I heard. But Mr. Conley's eyes lit up at that. He started asking more questions, but Richard was too sloshed to make much sense. Kept talking about puzzles and recovery phrases. Oh, at one point he did go on a rant about how you can't trust people. Said something like 'Even those closest to you will stab you in the back if enough money's involved. Then he mentioned his wife. Talked about how she was the only one he could trust. Said she was the love of his life." A wistful expression crossed the bartender's face. "You could tell even drunk off his ass, the old bugger really loved his wife. Kept going on about how he missed her."

"He also made some cryptic comments about his money," Jaime continued. "Said the old way of buying gold bars and stashing them was foolish. Mentioned something about digital gold?" He scratched his head. "I didn't really understand that part. But he clearly had some unusual ways of protecting his wealth."

Carson's eyes lit up with realization. "Digital gold… I think he was talking about cryptocurrency. Bitcoin, specifically. That would make sense as he was talking about recovery phrases." But he was met with blank stares from Destiny and Jaime and attempted to explain the concept.

Destiny furrowed her brow at Carson's explanation of the intricacies of cryptocurrency and digital wallets. As someone who preferred the tangible feel of cash in her pocket, the concept of storing money digitally in encrypted codes seemed abstract and dubious to her.

"So let me get this straight," she said slowly. "This Richard guy basically converted a bunch of his money into… digital coins?

That is stored in some wallet secured by a recovery phrase password?"

Carson nodded eagerly. "Exactly! The wallet contains the private keys needed to access the cryptocurrency funds. The recovery phrase - usually 12 to 24 words - allows you to restore the wallet if your device gets damaged or lost. So whoever has that recovery phrase has access to the money."

Destiny shook her head in disbelief. "That sounds way too risky. What if you lose the device and forget the recovery phrase? Wouldn't the money be lost forever?"

"Yes, that's why they recommend carefully storing the phrase somewhere secure like a safe," Carson explained. "Losing your recovery phrase is essentially like losing the keys to a safe containing your money."

Comprehension slowly dawned on Destiny's face. "Oh, I get it now. So Richard had somehow hidden away a crypto fortune. How big of a fortune are we talking about? Big enough to potentially motivate murder?"

She and Carson looked at one another, a silent acknowledgment passing between them as the same realization seemed to strike. They turned to Jaime, who was polishing a glass behind the bar.

"Jaime," Destiny said. "What more can you tell us about Richard's death? We know it happened sometime after Christmas that year, but do you remember any details surrounding it?"

Jaime frowned, setting down the glass and rag. "Officially it was marked down as natural causes. Old guy with a history of asthma and other health issues. I wish I could tell you more. But the whole thing was kept pretty hushed up. All I know is he died in his room sometime between Christmas and New Year's."

He lowered his voice. "There were rumors going around that it wasn't reported right away. His body was already cold by the time they contacted the authorities. But that's just gossip from the staff."

Carson and Destiny shared a knowing look. The timing was certainly interesting, given Richard's apparent crypto wealth and Lance Conley's odd behavior leading up to his own death the following Christmas. Too many coincidences to ignore.

Jaime shrugged. "I wish I could tell you more. But that's about all I know about Richard McDowell. Hopefully, it provides some kind of lead."

"It definitely gives us some new angles to consider," Carson said. "We really appreciate you opening up about this, Jaime. It's invaluable to piecing this mystery together."

Jaime managed a small smile. "I just hope it helps put Richard and Mr. Conley to rest, along with all the strange things happening around here."

Chapter Eleven

Destiny and Carson stepped out of the cozy hotel bar, both lost in thought as they processed the revelations Jaime had shared about the late Richard McDowell.

"Well, that was certainly enlightening," Carson finally said, breaking the silence. He turned to Destiny with an amused smile. "We make a pretty good mystery-solving team, don't you think?"

Destiny laughed. "Like good cop, bad cop?"

They stood facing each other for a moment, both suddenly unsure what to say next. The lobby was quiet now, with only a few staff and guests passing by. Twinkling lights from the towering Christmas tree cast a warm glow over them.

"I should probably head home and get out of these muddy jeans," Destiny said, tucking a strand of hair behind her ear self-consciously. "But this was... nice. Spending the afternoon together, I mean."

"I had a really great time today," Carson said sincerely. "You're incredibly talented, Des. Filming you was...magical."

Destiny flushed at the unexpected compliment. "It was fun. Crazy, but fun." She hesitated. "Thanks for believing in me."

Impulsively, Carson reached out and squeezed her hand, his rough palm enveloping her slender fingers.

"Today was only the beginning," he looked into the depth of her soul.

Destiny's heart swelled at his words. For once, she let herself believe that anything was possible.

Slowly, Carson released her hand, though his gaze still held hers.

"Drive safe," he said. "See you tomorrow."

ON HER WAY towards the lobby, she decided to take a quick detour to see if her mentor was still around.

Pushing through the double doors, Destiny spotted Kari sitting at one of the dining room tables with a cup of tea, focusing intently on her tablet.

"Hey Kari, sorry to bother you if you're busy," Destiny said as she approached.

Kari glanced up, her piercing blue eyes softening when she saw it was Destiny. "No bother at all, kid. Just finishing up some inventory. What's going on?"

Destiny pulled out the chair next to Kari's and sat down. "Well, Carson and I were just talking to Jaime the bartender about that guest who died here a couple of years back. Richard McDowell? Jaime had some interesting info about the guy."

"Oh yeah?" Kari raised an eyebrow. "Like what?"

"Like the fact that he and Lance Conley apparently had some drunken conversation about cryptocurrency right before Richard died," Destiny leaned forward and said in a low voice. "Apparently Lance was really interested in the recovery phrase for Richard's crypto wallet."

Kari let out a low whistle. "Well isn't that a pip. Definitely worth obsessing over."

"Right?" Destiny agreed.

"What else did you find out?"

"That's about it from Jaime. Oh, but there is something I want to ask you. I had a run-in with the Clydesdale carriage today and the carriage brothers mentioned something to me. Did anything strange happen here in the kitchen or hotel on Christmas Eve two years ago?" she asked.

Kari paused, thinking back. "You know, now that you mention it, that was the first time I experienced something really weird here," she said slowly. "Although at the time, I figured it was just some newbies messing stuff up."

"What happened?" Destiny asked eagerly.

But before Kari could elaborate further, a loud crash echoed from the other side of the kitchen, followed by shouting.

Kari rolled her eyes and sighed. "Speaking of. I can't tell anymore if it's the ghost or Fumbles McButterfingers strikes again." She stood up and tucked her tablet under her arm. "Call me later tonight and I'll tell you more about it," she told Destiny. "I gotta go, duty calls."

With an apologetic smile, Kari hurried off to deal with the commotion in the kitchen, leaving Destiny sitting there, curiosity unsated but even more intrigued by this new lead. It seemed Christmas Eve two years ago had been even stranger than she realized. She made a mental note to call Kari later that evening to get the full story. For now, it sounded like the head chef had some chaos to rein in.

As Destiny unlocked her front door, Velvet came bounding over, purring and rubbing against her legs in an affectionate greeting.

"Hey there, Velvet meow," Destiny said, bending down to scratch the cat behind her ears. Velvet's presence always soothed her, and after the strange events of the past few days, the comfort of home and her feline friend felt especially welcoming.

Destiny heated some homemade ginger butternut squash soup and drizzled some truffle oil in, one of her favorite comfort foods, and settled onto the couch with Velvet curled up beside her. As she ate, her thoughts drifted to Carson. She smiled remembering their playful snowman building and stargazing, the way his smile made her heart flutter when their eyes met across the dinner table. With the way things have been intensifying at the hotel, it felt like ages since she first met him in the gift shop, while it had only been five days.

With a sigh, Destiny set down her empty bowl, emotions swirling inside. Part of her longed to fall for Carson, to experience love again after so much heartbreak. But painful Christmas memories flashed through her mind - Patrick breaking up with her in the Ferris wheel cabin on Christmas

Day, her skiing accident that ruined Christmas, and getting fired on Christmas Eve. She couldn't risk that kind of hurt, not again. Especially not at Christmas, a time already weighted with grief and disappointment.

Velvet nuzzled Destiny's hand, purring. The gentle contact eased Destiny's sadness. That was enough for today. She decided to run a bath, her bruised knee and sore body could use a good soak right about now.

Destiny sank into the steaming bathwater with a contented sigh, the scent of lavender and eucalyptus soothing her weary body. She leaned back, wet hair piled atop her head, and tried to empty her mind after the eventful day. Alas, questions still nagged at her consciousness. Reaching for her phone on the bath's ledge, she scrolled to Kari's number and hit call.

The phone rang twice before Kari's voice answered. "Hey Des."

"Hey, Kari. I hope I'm not catching you at a bad time."

"I've always got time for you. Besides, we have an unfinished conversation to catch up on."

Kari recounted the strange events from two Christmases ago to Destiny over the phone.

"Right in the middle of the eight o'clock dinner rush on Christmas Eve, a whole shelf of plates came crashing down and smashed into a billion pieces on the floor. I had to get the whole front desk staff to help bring more plates out from storage. And because the weather was so bad, they had to use the horse carriage. I had a newbie on the staff who said he took a stack of plates out and caused the shelf to collapse, and took responsibility for the whole thing. But in hindsight, the poor guy was obviously just in the wrong place at the wrong time."

Kari said with a shiver. "We barely managed to get all the food out for the Christmas Eve dinner service. I'd never seen anything like it."

She went on to explain that even more frightening supernatural activities started up last Christmas, centered around the kitchen again. Utensils were somehow stuck up on the walls when no one was around. It got so bad that Seth decided to shut down the hotel just before Christmas, claiming renovations and maintenance issues.

"But the real reason was because it just wasn't safe with whatever was going on in there," Kari admitted. "We couldn't risk staying open."

After closing, Seth had apparently hired a shaman to come perform a cleansing ritual on the hotel. When they reopened in January, everything seemed back to normal.

"We thought maybe the shaman had banished whatever dark energy was plaguing this place," Kari said. "But now with plates flying and doorknobs rattling off, we were obviously wrong."

"But nothing weird happened throughout the whole year, it only started up on the day Carson and I came to the hotel?"

"That's right. The whole year was uneventful."

"Is it possible for a haunting to only occur around a specific time of year?"

"A seasonal haunting?" Kari was silent for a long moment. "I suppose.... don't see why not if there is some event tied to the spirit's unfinished business. It seems like whatever is haunting this place is only stirred up around Christmas. But Des, we mustn't obsess over darkness during this time of night. The night is for sleeping, healing, and dreaming."

She smiled, trusting her mentor's wisdom. "You're absolutely right. Thanks, Kari."

"Anytime. Now get some rest, and we'll tackle things fresh in the morning."

Destiny sank deeper into her lavender-scented bath, chilled despite the steaming water. She glanced up to see Velvet standing in the bathroom doorway, back arched, fur on end. The cat stared intently at something only she could see, making a chirping sound in her throat. Destiny's heart quickened.

"Velvet? What's wrong?" she called softly.

The cat's gaze remained fixated on the empty air, eyes wide. After a long moment, she turned and trotted out of the bathroom. Destiny sat up, water sloshing around her. She listened closely but heard nothing amiss in the old house. Still, she couldn't shake the uneasy feeling settling in her gut. Her cozy little home suddenly felt cold, and foreign.

Chapter Twelve

Destiny hurried to finish her bath. Wrapped in a bathrobe, she quickly headed out of the bathroom in search of Velvet. The cat emerged from under her bed, calmer but still on high alert. Destiny scooped Velvet into her lap as she settled on the bed.

"It's okay, sweet girl, we're safe," she murmured, stroking Velvet's soft fur. The cat nuzzled against her but kept glancing around the room as if tracking phantom movements.

Destiny's mind raced, thoughts returning to her conversation with Kari. Could a dark presence have followed her home from the hotel? She shivered, holding Velvet close. As much as she wanted to dismiss it as paranoia, Destiny knew to trust her intuition, and Velvet's instincts especially. Something was amiss.

Her gaze fell upon the cat treats lined up neatly on the floor. Destiny felt as if the blood in her veins had frozen - she certainly hadn't arranged them that way. As she watched, another treat slowly slid across the floor to join the formation. Velvet hissed, fur bristling.

Destiny's heart drummed a rapid rhythm against her ribcage as she followed the trail of cat treats leading to the Christmas tree. Each step seemed to echo in the quiet of her living room, a stark contrast to the storm of unease brewing within her. The festive lights of the tree cast a warm glow, but the cozy comfort they usually offered had been snatched away by the eerie sight that met her eyes.

Every one of Velvet's toys, normally scattered across the floor in disarray, now adorned the branches of the tree like bizarre ornaments. They hung there, swaying slightly, as if an invisible hand had just finished placing them. Destiny's breath hitched at this violation of her home, her sanctuary.

A soft mew from Velvet drew Destiny's gaze upward. The cat was fixated on something above, her wide eyes reflecting fear and fascination. Destiny followed Velvet's stare but saw nothing more than the stucco expanse of her ceiling. The air grew thick with silent tension; even though she couldn't see anything, she could feel an oppressive presence pressing down on her.

Velvet's fur stood on end, and she backed away from the tree with her funny chirping sound. Destiny felt a chill skitter through her despite the robe wrapped tightly around her. The warmth from earlier had evaporated into a cold dread that settled in her bones.

With a pang, she realized her home was no longer her safe haven insulated from the otherworldly forces at play. The phenomena from the hotel had breached her threshold, crossing into her personal space with chilling audacity. The ghost or whatever malevolent force was at play, was here now, sending a clear message. It knew her, knew where she lived, and it was capable of reaching into the very heart of her sanctuary.

Velvet suddenly darted under the couch, seeking refuge from whatever hung unseen in their midst. Destiny swallowed hard against the lump forming in her throat and reached for her phone with trembling fingers. Embarrassing or not, it was time to seek help.

CARSON LAY SPRAWLED across the hotel bed, a crumpled notepad and pen beside him. Clues and observations were scribbled across the pages in a chaotic whirl of ink—evidence of his attempt to piece together the mystery that wrapped around Christmas Hills like a thick fog. But for all his efforts to focus, his mind kept veering down a path less analytical and more... personal.

Destiny's image floated into his thoughts unbidden, her hazel eyes wide with fear and determination. He remembered their first encounter, how she'd sparkled with that same intensity even as she'd tried to ward off the pull of attraction. A smile played on his lips at the memory, how fate seemed to weave their lives together with threads named coincidence—or perhaps, destiny.

A sigh escaped him as he recalled his icy mishap on the road. The rental company had dealt with the car situation, saving him from a frosty headache. He still couldn't shake the image of the tree he'd hit—strangely alone in an open space, as if it had been waiting for him.

His phone's ringtone shattered his musings, yanking him back to the present. He reached for the device with a frown, irritation mingling with curiosity. Who would call at this hour?

THE RINGING on the other end seemed to vibrate through the tension in the air. When Carson's voice finally cut through, it was a lifeline amidst churning waters.

"Carson, it's Destiny. I think... I think I'm getting too close to something here," she started without preamble, voice wavering slightly despite her best efforts to sound composed.

On the other end of the line, Carson sensed the urgency threading through her words. "Destiny? What happened? Are you okay?" His concern laced every syllable, mixing with curiosity and an edge of protective instinct.

She glanced at the eerily decorated tree and swallowed back the panic that threatened to overtake her calm exterior. "No, not really. My house—it's been... touched. Things are moved around in a way I can't explain. It feels like a warning."

"A warning?" Carson echoed, sitting up straighter where he lounged on his hotel bed. His mind raced as he pieced together what little she'd revealed.

"Yes," Destiny affirmed, stealing glances at Velvet's hiding spot. "Like whatever's haunting the hotel knows I'm onto it and is trying to scare me off."

Carson ran a hand through his hair—a nervous habit he couldn't shake when worry crept in. "I'll be right over," he declared with no hint of hesitation.

"No—Carson, you don't have to—" Destiny began to protest but stopped short as another cat treat skittered across the floor toward its mates.

"I do have to," Carson interrupted firmly. "I'm not leaving you alone with... whatever this is."

She let out a breath she didn't realize she'd been holding and conceded with a small nod even though he couldn't see it. "Okay," she murmured. "Okay."

CARSON ENDED THE CALL, his heart thumping against his chest like a frantic drummer. He stood, pacing the length of his room as a sense of urgency clawed at him. Destiny needed him — she was scared, alone, and whatever was haunting Christmas Hills had infiltrated her home. He had to get to her.

A glance at the digital clock confirmed the lateness of the hour. The rental car company had taken his mangled sedan away earlier, leaving him stranded at the resort without transportation. He muttered a curse under his breath and grabbed his coat as he hurried out the door.

The lobby of the Christmas Hills Resort was quiet, save for the soft hum of holiday music and the gentle crackle of the fireplace. Vincent stood behind the front desk, a book in hand, looking every bit the consummate professional despite the late hour.

"Vincent," Carson called out, approaching with swift strides.

The front desk worker looked up, eyebrows lifting in mild surprise. "Mr. Akin, what can I do for you?"

"I need to get to Destiny's place, right now," Carson said, urgency etching his voice. "Is there a taxi or something I can call?"

Vincent set his book aside, adjusting his glasses as he assessed Carson's anxious demeanor. "I'm afraid no taxis are running at this time of night in Christmas Hills," he replied with a sympathetic tilt of his head.

Carson's shoulders sagged slightly, but Vincent was already reaching for the phone. "However," he continued, "I may have a solution."

Vincent dialed with practiced ease, speaking in hushed tones into the receiver. After a brief exchange and several nods, he hung up and faced Carson again.

"One of the Carriage brothers will take you," Vincent announced with a small smile playing on his lips. "They're night owls and always happy to help out."

Carson let out a breath he hadn't realized he'd been holding and nodded his thanks. "How long will they be?"

"They're just finishing up some work on their farm nearby," Vincent assured him. "They should be here shortly."

True to Vincent's word, within minutes a pair of headlights cut through the darkness outside as an old pickup truck pulled up to the resort's entrance.

"Need a lift?" Freud called out as he approached Carson.

Carson couldn't help but offer a grateful smile despite his worry. "More than you know," he said.

The truck rumbled through the crisp night, its headlights cutting a swath through the darkness. Carson settled into the passenger seat, tucking his hands into his coat pockets as he cast a glance at Freud.

"Really appreciate this late-night ride, Freud. "

Freud's chuckle resonated in the small space "Well, Carson, it's not unheard of around here. At least it's not like two o'clock in the morning like on Christmas Eve two years back — quite the night."

Carson leaned forward. "Yeah, you mentioned that. What happened?"

The truck hit a pothole and jostled them both before Freud continued. "Blizzards stacked up one after another that year. Felt like the sky had a grudge against us. Then, right when everyone's all cozied up after the Christmas Eve Feast, the hotel's boiler goes kaput."

Carson raised an eyebrow. "That sounds... unfortunate. The whole hotel?"

"Luckily not, just one wing," Freud said with a nod. "Guests were freezing in their rooms. The hotel was fully booked so Mr. Conley didn't have a single spare room to offer the guests to switch to, so he had no choice but to call Pat for space heaters."

"How many did you end up getting?"

Freud tapped his fingers on the steering wheel as if counting. "Thirty heaters—three for each of the ten rooms in that southwest wing on the first floor."

Carson sat up straighter. "That's my wing. But there's twelve rooms."

"Yep," Freud replied, glancing over, "heaters for all except for the first two rooms."

A thoughtful look crossed Carson's face. "Funny, I'm staying in one of those rooms."

Freud gave him a sideways glance and quirked an eyebrow. "Warm enough for you?"

Carson chuckled. "Mine's fine, but I'd say the room across has seen better days."

The truck's engine growled to a halt in front of Destiny's house, the beams of the headlights dimming as Freud put the truck in park. Carson reached for the door handle, giving the cabin a once-over before stepping out into the chill of the night.

"Thanks for the lift, Freud," Carson said, his breath forming a misty cloud as he spoke.

Freud waved a hand dismissively, a wry smile tugging at his lips. "No trouble at all. Wouldn't want you walking in this cold."

Carson shut the door with a soft thud and turned to face Destiny's home. It stood like a warm beacon against the stark backdrop of the snowy night, windows aglow with inviting light. He glanced back at Freud, who was already rolling away.

"Just give me a holler if you need another ride," Freud called out, his voice muffled slightly by the knit scarf wound tightly around his neck.

With a nod and a grateful smile, Carson watched as Freud's truck pulled away from the curb and rumbled into the night like an old bear.

Chapter Thirteen

The door swung open before Carson could knock, revealing Destiny in the warm glow of her living room, her face a canvas of distress. Clutched to her chest, Velvet offered a pair of wide eyes that seemed to mirror her owner's concern.

Carson stepped inside, the chill of the night surrendering to the cozy warmth enveloping Destiny's home. His gaze fell upon the Christmas tree, a chaotic blend of traditional decorations and... cat toys? They dangled among the branches, a bizarre twist to the festive adornments.

"Seems Velvet's been moonlighting as an interior decorator," Carson quipped, aiming for levity in the thick air of unease.

Destiny forced a weak smile, the tension in her shoulders betraying her attempt at humor. "I wish it was just her going on a redecorating spree." Her voice wavered as she set Velvet down, who immediately began pacing with an unusual sense of purpose.

He stepped closer to inspect the tree. The catnip mice and jingle ball ornaments still winging subtly.

"Looks like she's got quite the artistic eye," he continued, glancing back at Destiny with a playful raise of his brow.

Destiny wrapped her arms around herself, the shivers that ran down her spine only partially from the cold. "I think the ghosts from room 1302 have decided to follow me home," she said, her voice tinged with a mix of fear and disbelief. Her gaze lingered on the Christmas tree as if expecting it to confirm her suspicions.

Carson's expression softened, the humor fading into genuine concern. "I'll stay over, keep watch if that'll make you feel better," he offered, stepping into the role of protector as naturally as if it were second nature. "Don't worry, I'll take the couch."

Relief washed over Destiny's features like the first rays of dawn dispelling night's shadows. "Thank you, Carson," she breathed out, grateful for his reassuring presence.

Moments later, she returned from the linen closet armed with two sets of duvets and pillows, a determined glint in her eye. "You take the long side of the L-shaped couch," she instructed, dropping one set onto the cushions with a decisive fluff. "I'll take the short side."

She straightened up and flashed him a brave smile. "Might as well make a fun sleepover out of it, right? Like telling ghost stories over a campfire, with hot cocoa." She hurried to the kitchen, grateful for the distraction of preparing hot cocoa. The familiar motions soothed her rattled nerves as she warmed the milk, and added chocolate, and a dash of cinnamon. Soon the cozy scents of chocolate and spice filled the kitchen, transporting her to childhood nights nestled by the fire with her family.

Carrying two mugs piled high with whipped cream and marshmallows, Destiny rejoined Carson in the living room. He accepted the steaming drink with a smile.

"So I spoke with Kari earlier about the weird stuff that's been going on," Destiny started, taking a tentative sip. Carson nodded, his expression intent as he listened. She recounted everything Kari had shared - the first kitchen haunting two Christmases ago, the peculiar occurrences leading up to the hotel's temporary closure last year, and the shaman's attempted cleansing ritual.

"If this really is some kind of seasonal haunting, there must be a specific trigger," Carson mused after she finished. "Something tied directly to the holiday itself."

Destiny nodded slowly. "You're right. We know Richard McDowell died two Christmases ago. And Lance Conley died last Christmas when problems resurfaced."."

"Exactly. If either of their deaths involved foul play..." Carson trailed off, eyebrows knitting together.

"It would make sense as a catalyst for paranormal activity," Destiny finished, mirroring his pensive expression.

They sipped their cocoa in silence for a few moments, turning over the possibilities in their minds. The warmth of the mugs seeped into their hands as the fireplace crackled soothingly, keeping the darkness and mysteries of the night at bay.

As THE FIRE danced and crackled, casting a flickering glow over the room, Destiny furrowed her brows in thought. The warmth from the mug in her hands contrasted sharply with the chill of the mystery that wound its way through her mind. She set the cocoa aside, her focus sharpening as she pieced together the timeline they had been given.

"There's something about the timing that doesn't quite add up," she said, her voice steady despite the haunting implications. "Kari mentioned the strange phenomena started on Christmas Eve two years ago, but that was before Lance Conley's death last year."

"Right," he agreed, "and Richard McDowell's death was shortly after Christmas, not before. If he died after the haunting incidents began, he couldn't have been responsible for them."

Destiny nodded, a sense of unease threading through her as they delved deeper into the unknown. "Unless Jaime remembered wrong," she suggested, considering every angle.

Carson's expression grew contemplative. He rested his chin on his hand, elbow propped on his knee. "It's worth digging into," he proposed. "We need to find out more about Richard McDowell's death—the exact time, date, and circumstances."

Destiny agreed with a decisive nod. "It seems like our best lead right now." She reached for her mug again, drawing comfort from its heat. "First thing tomorrow, we'll head to the hotel and start there."

With the lateness of the hour settling into her bones, she stifled a yawn. “Maybe we should change the subject before we drift off,” she suggested. “Don’t want any ghostly nightmares tonight.”

Carson nodded in agreement, taking a final sip of his cooling cocoa before setting the mug aside. He leaned back into the plush cushions, angling his body to face Destiny. "Good idea. We can pick this up again tomorrow." He paused, thinking for a moment. "So tell me — when did you first fall in love with cooking? What's the story behind that initial spark of culinary passion?"

A soft smile spread across her face as she delved into her memories. "I was maybe 10 or 11 years old. My parents were busy with the gift shop, so I'd spend a lot of time hanging around the bakery next door, watching them work their magic." Her eyes took on a faraway look, transported back to those childhood afternoons perched on a stool in the corner.

"Kari was working as a pastry chef there at the time. She must've been in her late teens, early twenties at the most, but for me she was invincible and I looked up to her. She took me under her wing, and let me help prep ingredients and decorate cakes. She was so patient, explaining techniques and chemistry of flavors and how ingredients pair together." Destiny chuckled lightly. "I think she saw how much of a sponge I was and wanted to nurture that interest."

She went quiet for a moment, her gaze drifting to the flickering fire. "There was something about the energy in that little kitchen. How ingredients came together and transformed into these incredible dishes. It felt...magical, in a way." Her voice softened on the last words.

Carson studied her face intently as she shared these treasured memories. He could envision a little Destiny, eyes shining as she peeked out from behind rows and rows of Kari's expertly constructed desserts.

"And now, learning from Kari again, it feels like I've come full circle," Destiny continued, meeting his thoughtful gaze. "Only this time, the magic feels more literal." She gave a small, incredulous laugh, still absorbing the revelation of Kari's supernatural lineage and the recognition of her own latent abilities.

As Destiny continued to reminisce, her words began to slow, slurring gently into a quiet mumble as sleep pulled her under its spell. Carson wanted to ask her more questions, but her voice trailed off mid-sentence, and her breathing deepened into the steady rhythm of slumber.

Velvet had been observing from a distance, but now she sensed the shift in energy. With feline grace, she padded over to Carson's side of the couch. The cat assessed him for a moment with her big blue and green eyes. Then, as if deeming him worthy of trust and affection, Velvet hopped up beside him and curled into a compact ball of fur.

Carson felt an unexpected warmth spread through his chest as he looked down at Velvet. He gently stroked the cat's soft stripes, feeling an inexplicable sense of kinship with this small creature that had also found solace in his presence.

With Velvet's purring as a soothing lullaby, Carson allowed his own eyes to close. As he drifted off beside Destiny on their makeshift beds in front of the dying fire, it seemed that even amidst haunting mysteries and unearthed secrets, there could still be moments of simple peace and connection.

Chapter Fourteen

Sunlight filtered through the curtains, casting a golden hue over the cozy living room where Carson and Destiny had spent an impromptu night. As the morning's calm settled in, both stirred from their makeshift beds, nestled among cushions. Velvet, perched at the foot of the couch, fixated on a spot above them with wide-eyed intensity.

Destiny rubbed sleep from her eyes and followed Velvet's gaze to the ceiling, but saw only the smooth expanse of plaster. She frowned, a silent question forming as she observed her feline companion.

"Velvet's at it again," she murmured.

Carson propped himself up on his elbows, yawning. "Staring at ghosts?"

Destiny nodded. "It's rather disturbing."

He glanced around the room. "I'm starting to feel like we're on one of those ghost hunter shows."

"Except we don't have night vision cameras or ridiculous tech gadgets, and we need them." Destiny's gaze swept across the room and landed on a bizarre sight: Velvet's toys arranged in a neat circle on the coffee table, her treats piled in the center like some sort of offering.

Carson let out a low whistle. "Now that's new."

Destiny rose to her feet and collected Velvet into her arms. "This has to stop. I can't keep living with... whatever this is."

"Haunted cat toy circles? Yeah, it's not highly stressful." He stretched his limbs and stood up.

"I'm serious, Carson." She stroked Velvet's fur, seeking comfort in its softness. "I can't stay here if things are going to keep getting... rearranged."

Carson walked over to her, concern etching his features. "You could come stay with me at the hotel. They have room service."

A laugh escaped Destiny despite her worries. "And that's supposed to convince me?"

"It's not haunted room service." He offered a hopeful grin.

She shook her head with a smile that didn't quite reach her eyes. "Tempting, but I'll pass. My parents are just down the road. I can go stay with them later. But first things first."

"Right, we have a mystery to solve."

DESTINY ZIPPED up a small duffle with the essentials—clothes for the day, her trusty makeup kit, and an assortment of Velvet's favorite treats. She hoisted the bag over her shoulder and, with a last glance at her disheveled living room, locked the door behind her. Velvet, leapt into the backseat of the jeep, excited as always to go somewhere.

Carson settled into the passenger seat, rolling his shoulders to shake off the stiffness from his night on the sofa. As Destiny maneuvered the jeep through the winding roads toward the hotel, she couldn't help but feel they were being watched — probably just her imagination. Velvet gazed out the window, whiskers twitching in the sunlight.

The Christmas Hills Hotel loomed into view. They pulled up to the main entrance, and Destiny noted with unease that every staff member they passed offered them knowing smiles and sly winks.

Carson sighed as he caught a bellhop's exaggerated thumbs-up. "Looks like Freud's been busy spreading stories."

Destiny grimaced at the unwanted attention. "Small towns," she muttered. "You sneeze and someone three streets over blesses you."

"Awkward doesn't begin to cover it," Carson replied as he opened the door.

They continued through the hotel, enduring the shared glances and muffled giggles with as much grace as they could muster. The cozy warmth of Christmas Hills was now tinged with an uncomfortable transparency that neither of them appreciated.

VINCENT, ever the meticulous front desk worker, looked up from his neatly organized station as Destiny and Carson approached. The concierge's impeccable uniform was marred by a single splotch on his cuff — a testament to his accident-prone nature — but his demeanor remained composed.

"Good morning Mr. Akin, how may I help you?"

"Hey Vincent, We're looking for information on a previous guest."

"I'm not sure if I can do that, it's against our privacy policy."

"Actually, we're helping Seth Conley, and he said we would have the hotel's full cooperation." Destiny interjected.

"Just one moment while I call to confirm," Destiny and Carson nodded in acknowledgment as Vincent got on the phone and inquired in a low voice. He hung up after a few seconds.

"What's the guest's name?"

"Richard McDowell," Carson said, a sense of urgency lacing his words.

Vincent raised a finely arched brow but dutifully turned to his computer. His fingers danced across the keyboard with a fluidity that spoke of years spent managing guest affairs. The screen flickered as he navigated through the records, his eyes scanning lines of data before he paused and looked up with a discerning gaze.

"He checked in on December twenty-first, two years ago," Vincent began, his tone carrying an air of professional detachment. "But there's no recorded check-out date for Mr. McDowell."

Destiny exchanged a quick, tense glance with Carson. They leaned in closer as Vincent continued.

"The notes here are quite detailed." He adjusted his glasses, peering intently at the screen. "It seems Mr. McDowell required assistance contacting a local garage for car repairs and made reservations for one at our Christmas Eve feast."

"Anything about his stay? Habits? Requests? Allergies?" Destiny asked, hoping for more pieces to this increasingly complex puzzle.

Vincent nodded. "There was a nightly bar tab—always two Lagavulin 16-year single malt whiskies served neat — charged to his room."

"And which room did he stay in?" he inquired.

Vincent's finger traced a line on the screen before tapping it decisively. "Room 1301."

Destiny's heart skipped a beat. Room 1301 — Carson's current abode. Her glance shot up to his eyes, there was shock there, but she also saw a hint of amusement.

"Thank you, Vincent," Carson said, recovering from the news rather quickly. "You've been incredibly helpful."

"My pleasure, I'm here to help." Vincent offered them a polite nod as they turned away from the desk and stepped aside from the bustling activity of guests checking in and out.

Destiny whispered to Carson, "This changes everything."

Carson agreed with a nod, "Too bad, I'm going to have to eat my promise to you — it's haunted room service after all."

"That's what you're worried about?"

"Hey, my promises to you are important." Appreciating and smiling at Carson's reply, Destiny pulled out her phone, fingers flying across the screen as she typed out a text to Remy.

She gave a summary of their discovery — Richard McDowell had stayed in room 1301 two years ago, the same room that Carson was currently occupying. His records showed no checkout date.

Carson peered over her shoulder, reading the message. "We should mention the bar tab too," he suggested. Destiny nodded and added that detail.

Within moments, Remy replied, asking them both to come to her office in half an hour to discuss further. Destiny confirmed their attendance and slipped the phone back into her pocket.

Thirty minutes later, they made their way to Remy's office on the upper level of the resort. Destiny rapped her knuckles against the stately wooden door. "Come in," Remy's melodious voice called out.

They entered the office to find Kari, Remy, and Seth already waiting, with Benson seated at Seth's feet. As soon as Destiny and Carson took seats on the sofa, she let Velvet out of the bubble backpack and the two animals swirled around one another in greeting.

"Let's figure this out, shall we?" Remy clasped her hands together, her voice firm but not without warmth. "Time isn't on our side. The disturbances are escalating."

"We can't let this go on any longer, it's simply not sustainable to keep up with the kitchen's damages, not to mention the Christmas Eve Feast is going to be a disaster," Seth agreed.

Kari nodded, her sharp gaze flitting between each person in turn. "The sooner we settle whatever unrest plagues this place, the better."

Destiny turned, her eyes meeting Kari's. "So what are you thinking?"

Kari reached down to stroke Velvet's soft fur for comfort before locking eyes with Destiny. "Yes," she said firmly, then looked to Carson, "This time in your room where Richard McDowell stayed. Maybe we can reach him directly."

"Are we really going to do a séance in my room?" Carson's tone held a note of incredulity that was hard to miss, but one look at everyone around the room told him the answer to his question.

Remy stood up, decisive. "Then it's settled. Let's do it."

"Now?" Carson asked.

"There's no time to waste."

Carson exhaled slowly. "Okay then, let's do this," he said as he stood up and stepped toward the door.

Destiny scooped Velvet into her arms and followed him out, her heart thrumming with a mixture of fear and empathy for Carson.

Chapter Fifteen

The group reconvened in Carson's room shortly after. Candles cast dancing shadows against the drawn curtains and the smell of Palo Santo permeated the air as Kari prepared the seance table. Once the board and the planchette were in place, she took charge as she had before and instructed everyone to take their places around the table set up in the center of the room.

"Remember," she intoned as they placed their hands on the planchette, forming an unbroken circle of fingers on it. "Focus on positive intent and Richard's spirit and nothing else."

Destiny looked over at Velvet and Benson in their own chairs, both animals alert and apparently sensing the gravity of what was about to occur.

Carson glanced around at each face before settling his gaze on Kari. "And if he does show up?" he asked.

Benson let out a soft whine but remained still.

"We treat him respectfully," Kari replied. "We ask what ties him here and how we can help him find peace, and we offer to help him."

"And ourselves," Seth added quietly.

With a collective breath in and out, they steeled themselves for whatever might come next.

"Let us begin," Kari announced as she closed her eyes and started to chant softly in the ancient magical tongue, inviting Richard McDowell's spirit to join them in room 1301 – where his mortal journey had ended so abruptly two years prior.

The group collectively quieted their minds, preparing to open communication with any lingering entities. Carson placed his fingers lightly on the planchette, Destiny covering his hand with her own. As one, they took a deep breath and Kari uttered a single word:

"Speak."

The planchette trembled, then flew towards the letter 'R'. Everyone gasped as it continued spelling a name — R-I-C-H-A-R-D.

Remy leaned in. "It's him," she whispered and Benson whimpered. The spirit had answered their summons.

Kari's voice echoed softly, with a melodic incantation that filled the room with an otherworldly resonance. Destiny watched as the planchette beneath their fingers came to life, gliding over the board with unexpected force. The difference was palpable; unlike their last attempt, the answers now were not just clear but insistent.

"Richard who?" Destiny's heart pounded against her ribcage.

“M-C-D-O-W-E-L-L.” It moved so swiftly, that Carson nearly lost contact with it.

"What do you want, Richard? Why is your spirit not at rest?" Carson asked, his skepticism melting into genuine curiosity.

“X-M-A-S F-E-A-S-T. U O-W-E M-E.” The words formed one after another in rapid succession.

Eyebrows raised in collective surprise. Kari's mouth twitched in a restrained smile. "Have you been smashing my plates?"

“Yes.”

"Why?"

“W-A-N-T X-M-A-S F-E-A-S-T."

Kari scoffed. "Smashing plates doesn’t usually get you any feasts."

Silence fell over the group; even the planchette seemed to pause in thought.

"Did you haunt the kitchen, smash the kitchen plates, and do other weird stuff with the water and the sauce last year?" Destiny's voice was a mix of disbelief and amusement.

“Yes.”

"And two years ago?"

“Yes.”

"The bottle of Lagavulin 16 years in the bar, did you smash that too?"

“Yes.”

"Why?" Seth leaned forward, intrigued despite himself.

“U C-A-L-L-E-D N-A-M-E-S."

Carson chuckled. "You didn't like your nickname?"

"No No No No No No..." The planchette circled the word "No" on the board in fervent denial.

Destiny intervened with a soothing tone. "Ok. Take it easy. We didn't mean any disrespect."

The planchette quieted, and tension in the room lightened ever so slightly. Carson pressed on. "Can you tell us when you died?"

"1-2-2-4." The date struck a chord; they exchanged glances, realizing its significance — Christmas Eve.

"Do you remember how you died?" Kari asked gently.

"N-O H-E-L-P."

"What did you need help with?" Destiny pressed further, her brows knitted together.

"C-A-N-T B-R-E-A-T-H-E." Destiny suddenly remembered Jaime's tale of Richard's desperate inhaler puffs and felt a pang of sadness.

"Were you also responsible for making room 1302 icy cold and making creepy snowman modifications?" Carson's question was loaded with apprehension.

"No." The friends exchanged surprised looks; was there another player in this ghostly game? As the humans digested this new information, Velvet tilted her head quizzically from her perch by Destiny's side and started looking at the ceiling as if seeing invisible things again.

"Uh-oh," Destiny muttered under her breath and kicked Carson under the table to get his attention.

"If it wasn't you, then who was it?" Kari pressed on.

They waited for what felt like an eternity until finally, an answer came back to them.

“S-O-L-O-M-O-N-S."

Kari inhaled sharply, breaking the silence. Her unfocused gaze cleared as she looked at Remy. "The Solomons," she repeated.

“It appears new players have entered the picture. I think we should end our communication with Richard for now and discuss our next steps."

Seth said impatiently, "But we need to ask Richard... "

"We close this session," Kari's command was firm, resonating with the finality of a church bell at dusk.

With practiced ease, she performed the closing ceremony and then snuffed out the candles one by one. As electric light replaced the candlelight's intimate ambiance, Destiny's gaze wandered to Velvet. Her cat continued to scrutinize the ceiling with an intensity that made Destiny's skin prickle.

"What is it, Velvet?" Destiny murmured, though she knew the answer already.

Seth cleared his throat, drawing all eyes to him. "There's something I need to share with you all," he began, his voice hesitant. "Something I found among my father's possessions." Before he could elaborate, Benson issued a low growl that grew in volume as Velvet started making her peculiar chirping sound.

"M... Maybe we should continue this in Remy’s office," Seth suggested, eyes darting towards Benson as if seeking affirmation from his canine companion.

The group nodded in agreement, collecting their belongings and readying themselves to leave the room. Destiny cast a final glance at Carson's Christmas tree and felt her breath catch in her throat. Icicles hung from its branches like frozen tears—impossible given the warmth inside. Benson's growling intensified as if he too sensed the incongruity of their frosty adornment.

Destiny reached for Carson's arm. "Look at your tree," she whispered urgently.

Carson followed her gaze and let out a low whistle. "That wasn't there before."

The group moved en masse towards the door, Velvet trotting alongside Destiny while keeping her eyes fixed above them. As they filed out into the hallway, each felt a chill that had nothing to do with the room's temperature.

"THIS IS what I wanted to show you," Seth said as he entered Remy's office holding a leather-bound journal. "Found this among Dad's things," his voice a blend of reverence and discomfort. "It was Richard McDowell's."

They gathered around Seth as he opened the journal's aged cover to reveal the musings of a soul long departed. Destiny leaned in, her curiosity piqued as she scanned the handwritten entries.

"He writes about Emma a lot," Destiny began with a voice carrying a softness reserved for private revelations, her finger tracing the loops and whorls of Richard's writing. "Listen to this, June 17th: 'Emma would have adored the roses blooming by the fountain today. Their crimson hue matched her favorite dress, the one she wore the night I knew I'd love her until my dying breath.' She must be his late wife. You can feel how much he misses her."

Carson peered over her shoulder, drawn not just to the words but to the subtle dance of emotion on Destiny's face. He could see her empathy weaving through the script, binding her to Richard's yearning across the veil of life and death.

"But look here," Kari pointed out, tapping at a passage where Richard lambasted an incompetent contractor with biting wit. "He seemed to have hated everyone else with a passion. Certainly didn't hold back on his opinions."

The group chuckled, but it was edged with tension, knowing these were the thoughts of a man who still lingered in their midst as more than memory.

Destiny turned another page and cleared her throat, "November 3rd: 'Had dinner alone again at that blasted restaurant. The duck was overcooked, the wine mediocre. Emma spoiled me with her culinary gifts; nothing else compares.'"

"Sounds like he was quite the gourmand," Remy mused with a wistful smile.

"Here's another," Destiny continued, "December 24th: 'The holiday cheer grates on me. Emma's absence is a void no festive light can fill. Yet here I am, surrounded by couples reveling in their shared warmth.'"

Carson winced sympathetically; Richard's acerbic exterior had concealed a chasm of grief.

Destiny flipped through more pages, noting each mention of Emma. Then she paused, her brow furrowing. "Wait, there are words underlined throughout these entries."

She flipped back to the beginning of the journal to scan the pages more carefully, causing a slip of paper tucked between the worn pages to fall out. She crouched down to pick it up, revealing a sheet slightly crisper than the journal's own leaves. A series of words, each meticulously written in a different hand from the journal's entries, marched down the paper.

Seth leaned in, his face shadowing with recognition. "That's Dad's handwriting," he said, a trace of confusion threading his voice.

Remy reached for the paper, tilting her head as she read the words aloud. "It doesn't make any sense. Is it some sort of poem? Maybe a haiku?"

Carson chuckled softly, counting under his breath as his eyes followed the list. "Not a haiku," he corrected gently. "Haikus have seventeen syllables. There are twenty-two words here."

The group peered at the assortment of words that seemed to hold no rhyme or reason: 'Lighthouse,' 'Cobblestone,' 'Willow,' 'Revelation'... Random, yet purposeful; chaotic, yet precise.

"How very random," Remy mused.

Destiny studied the list again. The words felt like keys to an unseen lock, but what door they opened remained a mystery. "Maybe not random," she said thoughtfully then looked to Remy, "I need to borrow a piece of paper and a pen."

Destiny flipped to the beginning of the journal again and started to write down what seemed to be a random list of words.

"'Garden,' 'Mist,' 'Violet'... these are all underlined." Destiny's finger slid along the lines of text as she spoke each word aloud.

Carson leaned closer. "Do you think they mean something?"

"Could be important," Seth's gaze sharpened at the question, and Kari tilted her head, considering.

"Maybe it's some sort of code?" Remy suggested, hope threading through her words.

Destiny continued to scribble the underlined words on her piece of paper – 'Lantern,' 'Eclipse,' 'Whisper,' 'Lighthouse,' 'Cobblestone,' 'Willow,' – "Aha!" She stopped her scribbling with a loud exclamation as she recognized the words, making everyone jump.

"These underlined words in the journal," she said, voice laced with excitement, "they match the ones on this list—exactly. Here you have it. Lance Conley made a list of the underlined words inside Richard's journal."

The group leaned in, drawn to Destiny's conviction as if it were a beacon in the fog of their bewilderment.

"But why would father do that?"

"I'm not entirely sure, but what if these words are part of a crypto wallet recovery phrase?" Destiny proposed, her words tumbling out with an urgency that demanded attention. "Jaime mentioned how paranoid Richard was about his wealth —how he boasted about hiding things in unexpected places and digital gold."

Carson nodded, his analytical mind piecing together the scattered clues they had gathered. "A recovery phrase," he mused aloud, "typically has twelve or twenty-four words. But there are only twenty-two words here."

"And if Richard was as paranoid as we've been told," Remy added thoughtfully, "he wouldn't have kept all the words together. He'd scatter them to keep them safe."

Seth's expression shifted from contemplation to comprehension as Destiny's theory resonated with him. He could see the same obsessive determination that had consumed his father reflected in their own fervor to unravel this mystery.

"This must be what Dad was so fixated on during his last year," Seth said. "He was searching for these words, trying to piece together McDowell's hidden fortune." Then, suddenly the implications dawned on him and Seth found his throat constricted, as an emotional maelstrom of sorrow and disbelief threatened to swallow him whole.

"My father... was he truly reduced to this?" Seth's voice barely rose above a whisper, a plaintive note betraying the internal battle raging within him. "Chasing after a dead man's wealth? I grew up idolizing him, he was larger than life. And now... " Remy enveloped him in a gentle hug, muffling his soft monologue.

Carson stepped forward, his earlier humor subdued into something more contemplative. "Seth," he began cautiously, "we can't jump to conclusions. We don't know anything for sure. Your father was the man who built a community here, whose hotel brought joy to so many. Let's stay positive and get to the bottom of this."

Encouraged by Carson's words, Seth turned to face the group, straightened his back, and nodded.

With newfound purpose solidifying their resolve, they began to strategize. "So far, we have twenty-two words that could be part of a crypto wallet recovery phrase and we need to find the two missing words," Destiny declared with a sense of authority.

"We need to honor Richard's spirit by giving him the Christmas feast he demands," Remy added.

"And we can't forget about 'The Solomons,'" Kari reminded them. Her voice was steady but carried an undercurrent of caution—a reminder that there were still unknown variables at play.

The plan was clear: fulfill Richard McDowell's final wishes for a feast fit for his memory, unravel the mystery of 'The Solomons,' and chase down the elusive last pieces of a puzzle that could lead them to untold riches—or perhaps something far more valuable.

Seth looked around at the faces around him. "But we're swamped," he sighed.

Remy nodded, her thoughts mirroring her husband's. "We've got check-ins, guests flocking to the spa, a Christmas Eve Feast to prep, and half a dozen crises to avert before noon." She glanced at Kari, Destiny and Carson.

"Then what are we waiting for? We'd better get started," Carson said with a resolute nod.

"So it's settled then. Des and Carson can start with finding out who the Solomons were, and I will start working on two Christmas Eve Feasts simultaneously." Kari announced with authority, and the room filled with renewed energy as they gathered their thoughts and prepared for the tasks ahead.

"Destiny, a word before you head out?" Kari called out.

"What's up?" she asked, turning around to see the serious expression on Kari's face.

"We're running out of time," Kari said. Her eyes flickered with an intensity that hinted at the gravity of their situation. "Tomorrow is Christmas Eve, and I know that if we can't give the ghost what he wants tonight, tomorrow's dinner will be disastrous. We have one chance to get it right."

Destiny nodded solemnly. "I'll help," she said without hesitation. "What do you need?"

Kari's shoulders relaxed slightly at Destiny's immediate agreement. "I need your help to prepare the Christmas menu from two years ago — the one Richard would have had."

A mixture of determination and apprehension danced in Destiny's eyes as she accepted the task. "Consider it done," she said with quiet resolve.

"But there's more," Kari continued cautiously. "I have a way to let Richard become physical temporarily so we can talk to him — ask him about his journal." Her voice dropped lower, laced with warning. "This kind of magic dances on a fine line and can turn dangerous quickly."

Destiny felt a chill that had nothing to do with the drafty corners of the old kitchen. Magic had always been an abstract concept to her, but standing before Kari, she knew this was anything but make-believe.

"I'll need your help for that too," Kari finished.

"Of course, tell me what to do," Destiny replied without missing a beat. Her heart hammered against her ribcage not just from fear but from an eagerness to delve into the unknown realms that Kari navigated with such confidence.

"You can start off by getting some special ingredients for me," Kari listed off several items: an assortment of herbs; spices that weren't found in their pantry; roots and berries with exotic names.

"Where will I find all these?" Destiny asked, furrowing her brow as she committed each item to memory.

"You'll have to forage or procure from those who trade in such rarities. Luckily, Pat's general store is one such place, you'll find everything you need in the far back corner of his store," Kari said with a smirk.

As Destiny scribbled down the list of special ingredients, she felt herself being pulled deeper into an adventure she hadn't anticipated.

"Remember, we don't have much time," Kari reiterated as Destiny pocketed her list. "We must be ready by tonight."

Chapter Sixteen

In the polished expanse of the Christmas Hills Hotel lobby, with its grand hearths and festive adornments, Destiny and Carson approached the front desk where Vincent presided.

"Vincent, we need your help again."

"How may I be of service this time?" Vincent said, arching one of his over-manicured eyebrows.

"We would like you to search the hotel records for any guests named Solomon," Destiny said, her tone suggesting both urgency and a dash of hope.

Vincent peered at them through his thin-rimmed glasses, his brow creasing in concentration. "Solomon, you say?" He tapped at the keyboard with practiced precision, his gaze flicking between the screen and his visitors. "I'm afraid nothing comes up under that name in our current database."

Carson leaned forward, resting an elbow on the polished marble of the counter. "How far does the hotel system date back?"

With a slight tilt of his head, Vincent pondered. "Ah, yes. After old Mr. Conley passed away, we modernized our systems but retained financial records from the last decade for tax purposes."

"And before that?" Destiny inquired, her hazel eyes wide with anticipation.

Vincent's fingers drummed a silent rhythm on the desktop. "Those would be in hard copy, filed away. It will require some... archaeological effort." His lips curved into a wry smile at his own joke.

"We'd appreciate it if you could take a look," Carson said, offering Vincent a grateful nod.

"Of course," Vincent replied with a flourish of his hand as if to brush away any doubt of his commitment to this historical quest. "It might take me some time to dive into our records though, as you can see from the line of guests checking in...."

Destiny's smile softened her features as she thanked him. "We'll check back later this afternoon then." Turning to Carson, she asked, "What now?"

"Might be a good time to head to Santa Pats?" Carson suggested,

"Exactly what I have in mind."

THE CRISP MOUNTAIN air nipped at Destiny and Carson's cheeks as they strolled down Christmas Hills' Main Street, each step crunching on the fresh snow that had fallen overnight. Shop windows glowed with twinkling lights and garlands, their festive cheer spilling onto the sidewalks. Pat's General Store beckoned them with a promise of warmth and the sweet scent of cinnamon that wafted through its propped-open door.

As they entered, the chime of the doorbell heralded their arrival, and the cozy interior wrapped around them like a comforting blanket. The store was a wonderland of holiday trinkets and necessities, its shelves stocked with an eclectic mix that only added to its charm.

Santa Pat as the locals affectionately called him, stood behind the counter. Carson noticed his white beard had doubled in volume since the last time he saw him. His eyes sparkled when he saw Destiny and Carson approach.

"What brings my favorite people to Pat's today?" he greeted them jovially.

"I see you've been working on that beard!" Carson complimented.

"Ah, it's you! I hope you've been staying warm and enjoying our little town. Haven't needed to use the souvenir I hope?

"Well, we have actually."

"Oh, dear. How did it go?" Before Carson could reply, Destiny interjected gently.

"We're on a mission for Kari," her list unfurled in her hand like a scroll. "She sent us for some rather specific ingredients."

Pat picked up the list and squinted at it. "You're in luck, I happen to have everything on your list, and you can find them all in the far back corner. Big twin amethysts flanking the sides of that aisle, You can't miss it."

Destiny needed no further encouragement and was gone in a flash. Carson, however, remained at the counter.

"And while we're here," Carson said, "I was hoping you could shed some light on a bit of hotel history."

Pat leaned on the counter. "History? Now that's something I have in spades. What do you want to know?"

Carson leaned closer. "It's about the hotel heating problem two years ago."

Pat stroked his beard thoughtfully. "Ah yes, keeping schematics and records is crucial for these old buildings with their layers of renovations. Otherwise, you run into issues like old Mr. Lance Conley did."

Destiny's curiosity piqued. "Issues? What kind?"

"Well," Pat began, his voice dropping to a confidential murmur despite there being no other customers in earshot, "Mr. Conley had this notion to turn off the heat in one room and somehow managed to knock out the heat for the entire south-west wing."

"But why would he need to turn off the heat in one room?" Destiny walked up and asked. "Wasn't the hotel fully booked for Christmas?"

Pat shrugged, his broad shoulders lifting beneath his red sweater. "Hmm. I didn't think of that. That's a mystery for sure."

Carson pressed on. "How many heaters did you supply then?"

With a few clicks on his computer at the register, Pat pulled up an old invoice, peering at it through his half-moon glasses. "Let's see... thirty heaters it was. Three for each room across ten rooms in that wing."

The information hung between them like mistletoe waiting for acknowledgment. Carson exchanged a glance with Destiny; both were aware there are twelve rooms in that wing — and more importantly, why had Lance Conley disrupted an entire wing's heating during peak season for the sake of turning the heat off in one room?

"Thank you, Pat," Destiny said warmly as she handed the items she gathered around the store to have them rung up.

Carson offered his hand to Santa Pat. "Your insight is invaluable."

Pat waved off their thanks with a chuckle that echoed through his store. "Just part of being Santa around here—you get to know all sorts of things." He winked as they left, bells jingling once more as they stepped back into the chill of Christmas Hills with more questions than answers swirling in their minds.

The soft flurry of snowflakes greeted them like nature's confetti.

"I feel like there are some ideas that if I don't capture now I'd lose them forever. Can we find a place to talk through what we just learned?" Carson said with urgency.

"Me too, I know just the place." Destiny led them to the coffee shop on the corner, with its steam-fogged windows and promise of warmth.

Inside, the aroma of roasted beans and cinnamon infused the cozy space. They settled into a booth by the window, steaming cups cradled in their hands, providing a soothing counter to the chill that had followed them in.

Carson broke the contemplative silence first. "So," he started, tracing the rim of his cup with a thoughtful finger, "I'd bet those two rooms without heat were 1301 and 1302. But why?"

Destiny took a slow sip of her cappuccino, her eyes narrowing as she mulled over his words. "No one could survive without heating in winter here," she said softly. "Especially not during a blizzard. It's colder than a morgue." She paused, her gaze drifting to the window where snowflakes danced wildly in the wind. "Those rooms must've been unoccupied — or at least not by anyone living."

Carson nodded in agreement, his eyes meeting hers with an intensity that mirrored her own curiosity. "Exactly. And if we're right about Richard's ghost being our kitchen poltergeist for all three years... well, he would have had to be dead on Christmas Eve."

"But then why would Jaime insist he died after Christmas?" Destiny wondered aloud, her brows knitting together in frustration.

A lightbulb flickered to life in Carson's mind. "What if Mr. Conley turned off the heat in Richard's room to preserve the body? Keeping it cold might have been an attempt to avoid ruining Christmas with bad news."

Destiny leaned forward, her elbows on the table as she considered this angle. "That could be part of it," she conceded. "But what if there's more? What if Lance Conley was after Richard's crypto wealth? He might've needed time to find that recovery phrase before calling it in and having Richard's body and belongings removed."

They sat for a moment in shared realization before Destiny's expression shifted; a new theory was taking shape. "We need to find out who was staying in 1302," she stated firmly. "And I think I might know who it was."

The gears turned in Carson's head as he processed her confidence. There was something about the way Destiny said it that told him she was on to something big—something that could crack this case wide open.

SNOWFALL THICKENED OUTSIDE, blanketing Christmas Hills in a hushed serenity. Carson and Destiny returned to the hotel, a certain briskness in their step that mirrored the urgency of their quest. As they entered the lobby, Vincent spotted them and waved them over to the front desk, where he leaned forward with a conspiratorial air.

"I've got something you might find interesting," Vincent began, his voice barely above a whisper as if the very walls had ears. He shuffled through some papers and then presented them with a printout. "Financial records show a Mr. and Mrs. Solomon paid for a week-long stay starting December 19th, two years ago."

Carson's gaze sharpened as he took the papers from Vincent's hands. "That's right around the time when—"

"—When all those unexplained incidents started happening," Destiny finished for him, her mind racing.

Vincent nodded solemnly. "Exactly. But there's more," he added with a furrowed brow. "Their information isn't in our system anymore. I mean, it should be; we've got records going back ten years after the big digital update."

Destiny leaned on the counter, her curiosity piqued. "So you're saying someone erased the Solomons' records?"

"It seems so," Vincent replied, his meticulous nature clearly offended by such disorder.

Carson folded his arms across his chest. "Deliberately deleted... That implies someone didn't want us — or anyone — to look into the Solomons."

Destiny chewed on her lip thoughtfully before addressing Vincent again. "Do you remember any guests named Solomon?"

Vincent gave a slight shake of his head, an apologetic smile tugging at his lips. "I'm sorry, I'm not great with names unless they come attached to an incident."

"But Jaime might know," Carson suggested with a glint of optimism.

"Jaime?" Destiny echoed.

Vincent perked up at this. "Yes! Jaime has been here forever and knows everyone who's anyone at Christmas Hills Resort. If the Solomon went to the bar two years ago, Jaime would remember them."

The suggestion sparked hope between Carson and Destiny, and without another word, they turned and headed toward the bar.

When Destiny and Carson walked up, Jaime was lining up an array of different types of glasses and in the midst of scrutinizing them as a judge would the final contestants of a pageant.

He looked up as he heard the rhythmic clicks on Destiny's boots on the wooden floor as she and Carson approached. "Ah, just in time to taste the new batch for the Christmas Eve Feast," he said cheerfully, a welcoming smile on his face until he noticed their serious expressions.

"Not here for eggnogs, I take it?" He ventured a guess.

"Sorry Jaime, I'm sure they are to die for but.... " Destiny said, her voice gentle but firm. "We're running out of time. We need your help. Do you remember anyone named 'Solomon'?"

Jaime paused, staring intensely at his glassware ensemble as he searched his memory. A moment later, recognition flickered in his eyes. "Yes," he replied, "a cute little old couple. Drank a few glasses of wine at most, not heavy hitters. Must've been in their nineties. Both retired professors, no children. Loved animals." His face softened at the memory.

Carson leaned on the bar, impressed despite the urgency of their inquiry. "How do you remember all that from just serving them wine occasionally?"

Jaime rolled his eyes and shrugged as if it were both a blessing and a burden. "It's more of a curse really. I just can't seem to not remember random details — like how Mr. Solomon and Mrs. Solomon would carry around treats for any pets she met."

Destiny pressed on. "Did anything odd stand out about them?"

The bartender furrowed his brow in concentration but shook his head after a brief pause. "No, they were rather private people," he said slowly. "Didn't frequent the bar often—just a glass of wine here and there."

Carson watched Jaime closely, admiring his casual dismissal of what seemed like an extraordinary talent for recollection. "A curse or a gift?" he mused aloud.

Jaime let out a half-chuckle as he picked up a whisk. "Depends on the day," he answered wryly. "But mostly, it's just part of the job."

As Destiny and Carson walked side by side down the hotel's hallway, she couldn't help but notice the evolution of the hotel's Christmas decorations; the number of garlands and wreaths had more than quadrupled in the last week. However, the festiveness of the environment failed to warm her, as she was single-mindedly focused on their investigation and Richard's feast.

"Someone went to a lot of trouble to wipe out the Solomons' existence from this place," Carson said, his voice tinged with disbelief. "It's like they were never here."

Destiny nodded, her gaze distant as she sifted through possibilities. "And it had to be someone with access, someone who knew how to manipulate the system without leaving a trace."

They paused before an ornate tapestry depicting a winter wonderland, the threads woven with meticulous care, much like the plot they found themselves entangled in. Destiny's eyes narrowed as a thought struck her.

"What if it was Lance Conley himself?" she proposed.

Carson considered her words, weighing them against everything they had learned so far. "I agree, things are not looking good for Lance Conley as all arrows point towards him. But he's gone now," he countered. "We can't exactly ask him why he did it or what he was trying to hide."

"True," Destiny conceded, "but his actions might have set other things in motion—things we're still feeling today. In any case, we need to get to the bottom of it."

THEY ARRIVED at Kari's kitchen just as she was directing her staff with military precision, preparing for another busy evening of culinary excellence. The scent of baking bread and simmering sauces wafted out to greet them, a welcome reprieve from their intense deliberations.

"Kari," Destiny called out as they approached her mentor.

The chef turned from her post at the counter, "Have you found everything I asked for?"

"Yes, it's all here."

Kari's hands moved with practiced ease, accepting the bundle of peculiar ingredients from Destiny and Carson. Her eyes, sharp as a hawk's, scanned the items: dried henbane, aconite, lady's mantle, and vervain. "Where is the carnelian and howlite?"

"Oh yes," Destiny reached into her bag and handed over a separately wrapped package.

Kari nodded her approval, the ghost of a smile gracing her lips.

"Good work," she praised, setting the ingredients aside. "These will serve well for our purpose tonight." Her voice was a low murmur, nearly drowned out by the clamor of pots and pans clanging in the background.

Destiny and Carson exchanged glances, both feeling the weight of anticipation. The kitchen hummed with energy as Kari's crew bustled about, unaware of the spectral drama unfolding in their midst.

Kari leaned closer, lowering her voice to a conspiratorial whisper. "We'll begin after dinner service—9 pm sharp. Make sure you're not late." Her gaze shifted between them, locking onto each with a stern intensity. "And Destiny," she added, her eyes softening just slightly, "bring Velvet. Seth will ensure Benson joins us as well."

Carson's brow furrowed in thought. "How will this offering work?" he asked. His question hung in the air like steam from a boiling pot.

Kari straightened up and turned to face them fully, assuming the air of an instructor addressing her most promising pupils. "Tonight," she began, her voice steady and sure, "we'll present Richard with his Christmas feast—a ritual meal to appease his spirit."

She gestured to the ingredients laid out before them. "These are more than mere garnish; they're symbols with ancient power. We'll use them to create a bridge between our world and his."

Destiny nodded, entranced; she could almost feel the magic thrumming through the room — a subtle vibration that seemed to emanate from Kari herself.

"And after we've offered him his meal?" Carson inquired.

Kari's lips curled into a wry smile. "As he consumes his special feast, he will take on substance. When he has achieved a form substantial enough, we will proceed with our séance. Then it's the usual, we ask our questions, and hopefully he gives us answers that will help us to guide him towards peace."

Destiny took a deep breath. She trusted Kari implicitly, nevertheless, she felt both nervous and exhilarated at the prospect.

As Kari turned back to her chef personality — barking orders at a sous-chef who had overcooked the risotto — Destiny and Carson slipped away from the kitchen's heat and noise.

They walked through the dining room now bustling with early diners eagerly anticipating Kari's culinary masterpieces. The soft murmur of conversation mingled with the clink of cutlery against fine china—a symphony of normalcy that belied the supernatural undercurrents at play.

Carson glanced at his watch; time ticked away relentlessly toward their looming deadline.

"9 pm," he said aloud as much for himself as for Destiny or Velvet. "Let's hope this Christmas feast is one ghostly gourmand can't resist."

Chapter Seventeen

At precisely 9 pm, Kari, Destiny, Carson, Remy, and Seth gathered around an antique mahogany table, laden with a feast fit for kings or in this case, one perturbed spirit. As Destiny surveyed the elaborately set table, a swell of pride rose within her. They had transformed Carson's hotel room into a mystical dining hall brimmed with a warm, inviting ambiance.

Kari unveiled the first course with a flourish — a velvety lobster bisque, infused with white truffle oil. The delicate aroma wafted through the room as steam curled from the fine china bowls. "Henbane aids in bridging our world with the beyond, but is only suitable for the dead. For the living, it's lethal, and not a pretty death," she explained softly. The bisque's rich creaminess and tender lobster morsels made for an indulgent beginning.

Next came the salad course, a symphony of microgreens and heirloom tomatoes dressed in a white balsamic vinaigrette. "Aconite, though perilous in large doses," Kari noted, "heightens spiritual connectivity when properly harnessed."

The tangy dressing enhanced the freshness of the greens, each bite cleansing the palate and preparing them for what was to come.

The main course was nothing short of spectacular — a roasted goose glazed with honey and mandarin liquor. Its golden-brown skin glistened under the chandelier's soft light as Kari carved it tableside. "Lady's Mantle was a favorite of alchemists in the Middle Ages, they believed dews formed on the plant to be a vital ingredient in the making of the philosopher's stone. For our purposes tonight, it symbolizes protection and our intent to align with the best possible outcome for Richard, and ourselves." she shared.

"Is it also deadly poisonous?" Seth asked.

"No, this goose is too good to go to waste. I made sure it will be safe for us to have it if we feel like celebrating at the end of this evening."

For sides, there were pillowy mounds of baby potatoes topped with Raclette cheese and mushroom confit laced with Vervain, alongside urchin roe-flavored risotto sprinkled with Carnelian dust. Kari explained that Vervain promoted protection and peace while Carnelian was known to help spirits regain the ability to speak.

Dessert arrived as a showstopper — a panna cotta adorned with winter berries and a brittle caramel lacework that seemed almost ethereal in its delicacy.

"How did you make the shimmer on the panna cotta?" Destiny noticed an ethereal luminance and asked her mentor.

"Ground howlite powder. It helps to calm the restless, and connects lost spirits to the light," Kari answered.

The participants of the seance murmured in appreciation.

"Now, I must warn you," Kari continued with her gaze piercing through the dimly lit room. "Tonight, Richard's spirit will walk amongst us more tangibly than before. We must respect this boundary between life and death."

She proceeded to lay down the law of the evening. "Do not reach out to touch him unless he beckons. Do not provoke him either. Spirits often forget the strength they can wield in this plane with the help of magic."

The table was arranged in a precise formation, as Kari insisted on an order that would channel their collective energy most effectively. Destiny sat directly across from Carson. Remy and Seth flanked Kari at the head of the table.

Kari pointed to two plush seats reserved for Velvet and Benson who, perceptive as ever to the room's charged atmosphere, had taken their places without prompt. The pets seemed to sense their part in this otherworldly affair; Velvet's big eyes shone with an almost knowing glint while Benson sat alert and watchful.

"As for you two," Kari nodded at the animals with a hint of warmth softening her stern demeanor, "your senses exceed our own. You may perceive shifts before we do. Trust your instincts."

"Remember," she concluded with solemn clarity, "tonight's rite demands each of us to hold steadfast in our roles. We are here to offer Richard peace. Keep your hearts light and your minds clear. Fear clouds judgment and weakens our circle."

With a final glance around the circle, ensuring each member was mentally prepared for what was to come, Kari drew a deep breath and started to recite a spell in the ancient magical tongue.

The air grew still, the flicker of candlelight casting dancing shadows across the room. A hush fell over the gathering as a fog materialized out of nowhere. Then, as if woven from the very mist that curled around their ankles, Richard's form materialized at the head of the table.

He was a tall figure, bulky in stature with an imposing presence that filled the space. His attire was timeless — slacks paired with a dinner jacket. As he settled into his seat, his form wavered between translucence and solidity, like a signal struggling to find clarity.

With each dish that Kari presented, Richard partook in silence, his form becoming more anchored to their realm. The lobster bisque brought color to his cheeks; the salad seemed to solidify his hands as they moved with careful grace. By the time he sliced into the succulent goose, his once ghostly visage bore the robust complexion of life.

"It's been ages since I've had a meal like this," he said, his voice gaining strength and resonance. The timbre was deep and rich, tinged with a warmth that contradicted the nickname Jaime had given him.

Kari watched him closely, her expression unreadable yet intense. "How do you find the fare, Richard?" she asked with a cordial tilt of her head.

"Exquisite," he replied, a half-smile tugging at his lips. "Though I must admit, it's rather odd to be enjoying such delights without actual... physical hunger."

His eyes traveled over those assembled before him — a mix of trepidation and curiosity played across their faces. Carson leaned forward slightly, a look of intrigue etched into his features as he studied Richard's increasingly tangible form.

Destiny held her breath, blown away at how the ghost before them was able to enjoy Kari's feast — a sensory experience she had always associated with the living.

Remy exchanged a glance with Seth; both shared an unspoken acknowledgment of the extraordinary nature of this meeting — a chance to finally put the paranormal activities at their hotel to rest.

Velvet's ears twitched in response to Richard's deep voice while Benson remained quiet but attentive.

As dessert was served and Richard savored the shimmering panna cotta with visible delight, Destiny felt a sense of relief wash over her body. They've done it. He seemed pleased.

When Richard finished his last spoonful and laid it gently on the plate, his form was as solid as any living guest at the table. He looked up from his dessert with eyes now clear and bright.

"Thank you for this kindness," he said softly but firmly. "It's been too long since I've experienced such generosity." As he pushed back from the table and stood, the guests became acutely aware of the fact that Richard had moved the chair he sat in by at least a good six inches.

"Richard, if I may, we're all wondering about how you passed. Can you confirm what happened?" Emboldened by Richard's seemingly contented state, Carson, ever the pragmatist, was the first to voice the question that hung in the air like a charged cloud.

"Asthma," the ghost of Richard answered. "I was dressed and ready to go to the feast when I had an asthma attack. My inhaler fell and rolled under the bed. I phoned the front desk for help, but help never came."

"Are you sure you died before Christmas Eve?" Carson asked.

"What a strange question, of course. Else why would I regret missing my Christmas Eve Feast?" Richard's ghost gave him a sidelong glance.

"Richard, sir, the feast seems to have brought you some peace. Are you ready to let go of any grudge that's kept you anchored here?" Destiny asked hesitantly.

Richard looked at her with mild surprise etching his features. "What grudge?"

The group exchanged glances, they were relieved but also confused.

"But you must want something, Richard? You didn't hang out here all this time for a missed dinner? Why are you still here? How can we help you find peace?" Seth asked, a little too impatiently.

Richard's tone was genuinely puzzled. "That's what I wanted. My Christmas Eve feast. It was my last regret in life. My only regret in life."

"You don't have any other regrets? But you must, a grumpy man like you?" Seth asked again impatiently as a look of alarm came over Remy's face.

"It's precisely because I complained to my heart's content that I have no regrets. Had I not complained about everything I didn't like, I would be full of regrets now." Richard answered proudly, leaving everyone baffled and lost in this odd conversation.

Just then, Benson's low growl punctured the calm of the room. The small dog's hackles rose as he stared fixedly at a corner on the ceiling. Destiny immediately looked over at her cat and saw that Velvet was also staring at the ceiling, her big feline eyes locked on to something invisible to the human eye.

"Benson is sensing malintent," she said softly.

Richard followed Benson's line of sight and let out a heavy sigh that seemed to carry the weight of untold stories. "The Solomons are here," he stated matter-of-factly.

Seth shifted uncomfortably in his seat while Remy reached out to calm Benson who continued to growl at the unseen presence.

Kari leaned forward slightly, her tone measured but urgent. "Richard, do you know why they're still here? What binds them to this place?"

"I don't know, why don't you ask them yourself?"

THE TEMPERATURE in the room plummeted as Velvet's plaintive meows echoed off the walls. Kari's eyes narrowed. "Fine," she said, her voice cutting through the tension, "Since you don't want to help, I will invite them to share your feast."

"Hey! Why must I share everything with these pathetic mongrels?"

Kari ignored him and began to chant the spell. Something stirred in the air, and Destiny watched in awe as two forms began to coalesce above them. These spirits were starkly different from Richard's robust apparition. They appeared fragile and translucent, their outlines flickering like flames in a drafty room and their eyes were hollow pools of longing and sorrow.

“They seem so frail, and so..... sad,” Remy remarked.

"Not for long," Kari muttered under her breath and said what sounded like a command in the magic tongue.

The air grew so cold that frost began to form on the windows despite the central heating humming diligently through its vents. Richard looked on with a solemn frown and sighed loudly as he realized the Solomons were now eating from his feast.

Kari continued to chant, and as she did so, bit by bit, portions of the lobster bisque vanished - slices of honey-glazed goose, baby potatoes, the remains of the risotto. With each morsel, the elderly couple grew more substantial. Wispy edges firmed, foggy eyes sharpened behind owl glasses, faded wool coats taking on hints of their original color Soon they gazed around the table not as faded apparitions but almost fully manifested spirits, faint but undeniably present.

Finally, Mr. Solomon swallowed the last bite and looked up from the feast table, seemingly satiated. Recognition flashed across his face as he took note of Destiny and Carson with Velvet nestled between them. “Ah!” He exclaimed with muted delight. “The nice couple. With our little friend.”

At the mention of Velvet, Mrs. Solomon looked up, too, her spectral eyes shone like sunlit water. “Oh, Blossom! There you are,” she reached a trembling hand toward the white and gray cat. Velvet answered with a welcoming trill and trotted over to butt her head against the phantom’s fingertips.

Watching Velvet’s friendly demeanor with the Solomons, Destiny wondered how long her cat had been privy to the existence of the ghosts.

Kari asked gently, "Might you share how you came to be here?"

The Solomons nodded, gazing into some long-ago Christmas Eve. "We remember the Christmas Eve feast," whispered Mrs. Solomon. "Such lavish dishes, champagne toasts... " Her eyes misted slightly. "We retired very full and content."

Her husband patted her hand. "But I remember waking, feeling Fiona shivering beside me. I tried to warm her, but then grew so very tired..." His brow furrowed with the effort of recollection.

"The next thing I knew, I was looking at this darling girl," Mrs. Solomon nodded towards Destiny, "and our Blossom." Her expression became confused. "But how did we come to be here? Why can't I recall...?"

Destiny and Carson traded bemused glances. “When did you first see... Blossom?” Destiny asked carefully.

Mr. Solomon scratched his head. “A few days ago? We woke to find ourselves out there in the snow. We saw Blossom with her kind caretakers.” He gestured from Velvet to Destiny. “We tried to call out but had no voices. And no one could see us.”

Mrs. Solomon nodded excitedly. “But we could not leave our dear Blossom. So we followed to make sure she was happy.”

Understanding dawned on Destiny. “The scary snowmen and the cat toys in my Christmas tree, that was you?”

“Not scary, we made them smile!” Mrs. Solomon clasped her hands earnestly. “We wanted little Blossom to be happy and amused!”

“Her name is Velvet, not Blossom,” Destiny clarified.

“Her name may not be Blossom but no matter - we love her so, she looks just like our Blossom.” Mr. Solomon responded and beamed affectionately.

As the Solomons reached out to caress Velvet, Benson uttered a fierce growl. Kari eyed him curiously, then gazed back at the spectral couple with dawning comprehension.

"Your affection blinds you," she said sternly. "In clinging to the cat, you unintentionally tax her living energy."

The Solomons paled. "We only want her company!" cried Mrs. Solomon.

Kari nodded. "But she belongs to the realm of the living. What might we do to help you find peace? Would a proper burial give you comfort?"

The Solomons brightened at this. "Oh yes!" exclaimed Mr. Solomon fervently. "Somewhere peaceful, not right on the road where we have to hear the sound of cars all day long."

"And somewhere warm, like New Mexico where we're from," Mrs. Solomon added enthusiastically.

Her expression turned pleading as she gazed at Velvet. "But Blossom, won't you join us?" Mrs. Solomon implored, floating towards Velvet with arms outstretched.

Benson sprang in front of the cat, a snarling sentinel. Hackles raised, he snapped his jaws at Mrs. Solomon's wavering hands.

"Wretched little beast!" Mr. Solomon rasped. Making soothing noises, his wife beckoned more insistently to Velvet. "Come along, dear one..."

Face hardening, Destiny swept Velvet into her arms and backed away. "You cannot take her!"

Benson barked fiercely.

The ghosts pulled up short, crestfallen. Then Mrs. Solomon's gaze hardened. "Give us our Blossom!" she demanded, voice shrill.

Then it all happened too quickly. Benson lunged to get at the ghosts as Mrs. Solomon shrieked in rage. "I said SILENCE!"

With a sweep of her arm, one of the brass candelabra was levitated, and she hurled it wildly toward Benson. Just then, a blurry shape streamed out of Destiny's arms across the room and fell with a whimper as it collided with the candelabra aimed at Benson, sending both sliding across the floor.

"Blossom!" the Solomons shrieked. Rushing to Velvet's limp body, despair flooded Destiny's face as tears streamed down.

As Velvet lay motionless, Destiny choked back a sob. "She's barely breathing!"

The Solomons glided over, ghostly faces stricken. "Our sweet Blossom!" cried Mrs. Solomon. "What have we done?"

Kari spoke urgently. "She's just hanging on by a bare thread. As spirits, you can channel emotional and psychic energy to heal her." She met their anguished eyes. "But it may require all the strength garnered from our ritual."

The couple grasped hands, gazing down at Velvet's crushed form. Then Mrs. Solomon lifted her head, resolve steeling her voice. "We will give anything for our dear one." Beside her, Mr. Solomon nodded solemnly.

Kari bowed her head. "So you understand the cost?"

"We do," came the whispered reply.

Kari stepped back. "Concentrate on sending your essence into the cat."

The Solomons knelt beside Velvet, spectral forms glowing brighter and brighter. Their outlines grew diffuse as the supernatural radiance sank into the cat's body. Soon, what remained of the Solomons were but two glimmering sparks,

Just then, gently and silently, a tiny light showed up on the ceiling of Carson's room and quickly expanded into a brilliant light blue portal. The few remaining sparks in the room spiraled upwards into the portal before blinking out.

The assembled friends stared at the portal, stunned by the Solomons' selfless sacrifice.

Destiny held her breath, tears trailing down her cheeks. Then Velvet mewled faintly, lifting her head from Destiny's lap. A sob catching in her throat, Destiny cradled the cat close, pressing fervent kisses to her fur.

Around them, sighs of relief echoed. Carson wrapped an arm around Destiny's shoulders, grinning brightly through gleaming eyes. Kari and Seth exchanged triumphant smiles while Remy dabbed at wet lashes.

As Velvet revived, Seth glanced around. "What's happening with Richard?"

The ghost of Richard stood motionless by the Christmas tree in the room, entranced by the photo of a wedding ring that Destiny had printed. The once acerbic and cantankerous man now stood silent, a softness touching his features as he contemplated the image.

Kari approached gently. "Richard, you've enjoyed your feast at last. If it's true that you have no other regrets, what final needs must we address before you can rest?"

The ghost of Richard lifted his gaze, a trembling sigh escaping him. "Emma," he murmured, voice choked with longing. "I miss my Emma. So much. I'd be at peace if I could just find her... be with her."

"She's in the light, Richard," Kari assured him, her tone resolute yet kind. "You'll find her there; you need only step into it."

A shiver of trepidation coursed through Richard's apparition. "I'm scared," he confessed, a lifetime of gruffness melting away to reveal vulnerability. "After being so grumpy and mean... so selfish... I fear what might await me beyond."

"You have nothing to worry about," Kari said, her conviction bolstering his courage.

Richard's misty form blinked rapidly. "What if she won't have me? What if I made her wait too long? What if she's gone to heaven and I'm going to hell?" His lips twisted as he recalled his offenses. "I hoarded my money and spat at homeless kids. I was worse than that Grumpy Cat meme." Richard sighed heavily. "Let's just say I have centuries of apology bouquets to buy if Emma even lets me past the pearly gates for visitation hours..."

Kari smiled gently. "It is never too late for roses."

As if on cue, the tiny speck of light on the ceiling above them grew rapidly, blossoming into an iridescent orb that danced with life.

"Are you sure it's safe for me to go in there?" Richard's ghost asked Kari once more, and she gave him a reassuring nod.

Richard was just starting to drift upwards when Seth's plea anchored him momentarily. "Wait," Seth implored, and Richard paused to look back.

"What is it?" Richard asked.

"It's about my father, he obsessed over some things before he died. I don't think you would tell me, you might even get angry, but if I don't ask, I'll lose the one chance I have to understand what happened with my father the last year of his life, and if he went crazy or not."

Richard's ghost tapped his spectral wrist and rolled his eyes.

"My father spent his last days fixated on 24 words from your journal — we only found 22. Do you know where the other two are?"

A laugh, devoid of malice and filled with a strange warmth, echoed from Richard's lips. "Lance Conley was as mad as I was! Though not nearly as clever at hiding things." He leaned towards Seth conspiratorially. "Under the floorboard," he revealed casually.

Seeing everyone's shocked expressions, he laughed. "What, Jaime didn't tell you what a paranoid miser I was? I never trust the hotel room's safe, and your father's actions proved I was right to think so!"

Remy ventured carefully, "What should we do with it if we find it? Do you have any surviving family? Friends? Foundation?"

The light from above now cascaded around Richard like a celestial waterfall. He smiled — a genuine expression they had never witnessed before — and replied as he began to dissolve into the radiance: "Do what you will with it. Just keep your Christmas feasts amazing... and free for everyone." His form flickered in and out of existence as he added, "I've got enough in that wallet to feed a thousand guests for a century and more. Perhaps that will finally rid me of those dreadful nicknames."

And just like that, as his laughter mingled with the fading light, Richard McDowell was gone—his spirit released at last to join his beloved Emma in whatever lay beyond.

Carson gave a shaky laugh. "I've never seen ghosts before, let alone spirits crossing over into some mystical portal on the ceiling. And to top it off, this all happened right here in my room," He gazed at Destiny and Kari with newfound wonder. "You two are incredible."

Destiny tilted her head modestly but was spared by Kari's response.

"Nothing to it, pest control was all I was after. And of course, couldn't have done it without you all. You all did great with keeping your hearts open and your intentions strong. Now that one feast is over, it's time to prepare the next one, seeing as I'm already way behind. Destiny, want to lend me a hand with the closing ceremony to this epic seance?"

"My pleasure, Kari."

"How about lending me a hand in the kitchen tomorrow for the Christmas Eve feast, for the living?" Kari asked again, amusement dancing in her eyes.

Destiny gasped and hugged the unruffled witch.

Kari and Destiny raised their arms, chanting softly as everyone focused on restoring the integrity of the space in Carson's room. As the last echoes of the mystic language faded, Kari turned to the stunned friends with a serene yet knowing smile. "It is done."

"Well. That was... extraordinary." Remy sank into her chair, looking rather faint. Beside her Seth shook his head in awe, one hand absently stroking Benson.

“But there’s just one thing,” Remy continued, gazing up at where the Solomons and Richard had disappeared, “I wanted to help the Solomons with their last wish but,” she turned sorrowful eyes on the others. “Without knowing where their bodies are, we cannot even begin to honor our promise.”

Seth leaned over and gave Remy’s hand a squeeze. “It’s okay, honey, I too should have asked Richard which spot in the floor we should be looking. We’ll just have to do our best with what we’re given.”

"I... I believe I know the place.” To everyone's shock, all eyes shifted to Destiny and Carson as they said in unison.

Chapter Eighteen

In the soft glow of the laptop screen, Carson's fingers hovered for a moment over the keyboard before descending with purpose. A click resonated in the quiet room, and with that, Destiny's culinary website shimmered into existence on the digital landscape. Carson leaned back in his chair, a sense of satisfaction unfurling within him. He'd poured every ounce of his marketing expertise into this project, intertwining Destiny's passion for cooking with the enticing web design that now beckoned visitors to explore.

He scanned the homepage one last time, admiring how it captured Destiny's essence. High-resolution images of her delectable creations adorned the site, each dish seemingly ready to leap off the screen. Warm tones and rustic accents mirrored the cozy atmosphere of Christmas Hills, while elegant fonts and intuitive navigation promised a seamless user experience.

The thought of Destiny seeing it for the first time sent a wave of anticipation through him. He imagined her eyes lighting up, the way they did when they first met and serendipitously decided to help each other find their Christmas joy.

HE HAD one last piece of business before joining the Christmas Eve celebrations. Striding out into the lobby, he nodded at familiar faces bustling past, the atmosphere crackling with festive energy. At the front desk bedecked with holly garlands, Jaime gave a cheery wave while Vincent nodded in dignified approval, silver serving tray tucked under one arm. Carson felt a sense of belonging as a warmth that filled his chest. With a contented sigh, he rapped his knuckles lightly on the door marked “Manager’s Office” before poking his head inside.

"Knock knock, special delivery!" Carson breezed in, brandishing a festively wrapped box as four faces looked up with smiles. He blinked, suddenly self-conscious. "Oh I'm not interrupting, am I?"

"Not at all!" Remy beamed, rising to give him a one-armed hug, her other hand occupied with a champagne flute. "We were just rehashing everything that happened. Please," she touched his shoulder, guiding him towards the remaining empty seat between Seth and Destiny at the round table. "Join us."

Settling into the cushioned chair, Carson set his package on the table and accepted a glass of champagne from Seth with bemused thanks. He couldn't remember the last time he had sat chatting over champagne at — he checked his watch — just past one in the afternoon. But the bubbly effervescence perfectly matched the mood in the room.

"So, we were just discussing the sequence of strange events," Seth explained. "I must say, the details prove even more perplexing in hindsight." He shook his head before taking a sip of champagne.

Kari, standing calmly with arms crossed, merely arched one knowing brow. "I did try to warn you when strange incidents first began two years ago," she reminded Seth matter-of-factly.

He grimaced into his flute. "Yes well, warnings of supernatural forces seldom align with sound business strategies."

"We don't blame you." Remy rubbed her husband's shoulder. "In your position, who would have leaped to ghosts as the likely explanation?"

"Well," Destiny leaned forward, "at least now we can piece together the full story."

With an approving glance from Kari, Destiny inhaled deeply and began to unravel the tapestry of events that had led them to this moment. Carson sat beside her, his gaze supportive, while Kari's sharp eyes missed nothing.

"It started two years ago," Destiny said, her voice steady. "Richard McDowell happened to be driving through Christmas Hills when his car broke down. He couldn't get his car fixed due to it being the holidays and an unexpected snowstorm, and by his love for gourmet food found refuge here at Christmas Hills Resort."

Seth leaned forward. "So Richard was drawn by the reputation of our restaurant?"

Destiny nodded. "Exactly. Richard was stranded, but he was also looking forward to the Christmas feast prepared by Kari. But fate had other plans. Throughout Richard's stay here, he had frequented the bar nightly. On one of these nights, he shared a drunken conversation with Seth's father and revealed he had a crypto fortune hidden away. A few days later, while anticipating the Christmas Eve Feast, he had an asthma attack in his room. His inhaler rolled under the bed, he phoned for help, and the call was answered by none other than Seth's father at the front desk."

Remy tilted her head. "But why was Seth's father answering phones at the front desk?"

"Because earlier that day, the Clydesdale brothers lost control of their carriage in the blizzard and almost ran Vincent over. Vincent broke his arm and had to go to the hospital, and Seth's father had to fill in as there was nobody else. So, getting back to our mystery, Christmas Eve was a very busy day at the hotel, at full occupancy and one employee short. Seth's father answered the distress call from Richard, but he got distracted with flocks of guests checking in and wasn't able to immediately make it to help him. By the time he arrived at 1301, Richard was already dead."

"And there's my father's involvement," Seth added grimly.

"Yes," Destiny agreed. "Lance Conley knew about Richard's wealth in cryptocurrency and decided on the fly to open the safe to see if he could find anything. He found Richard's journal and decided to keep it. Furthermore, he decided not to report the death right away, possibly because he wanted more time to look around Richard's belongings, possibly because he considered it bad press to have a guest's death on one of the most festive days of the year. Later that evening, he thought it would be a good idea to turn the heat off in Richard's room so as to mask the time of death, but there was a problem with the hotel's boiler system and the heat was turned off for the entire southwest wing. Soon after, the hotel started getting calls from guests who felt cold. Realizing his mistake but not wanting to turn the heat back up, Richard decided to get space heaters for the guests in the southwest wing. This is when things went terribly wrong."

"The old couple who died because they were left in a freezing room," Seth interjected with a wince.

"Yes," Destiny continued, "Tom and Fiona Solomon were staying in the room adjacent from Richard's. They were in their nineties, and the hypothermia killed them rather quickly. I believe Lance Conley knew about their deaths right away, as reflected in the number of heaters he ordered from the general store. Lance Conley knew he would get into deep trouble, not to mention really bad press for the hotel if it was found out that he froze his guests to death. He knew that Tom and Fiona Solomon were alone in the world and wouldn't be missed, and did the unthinkable: he buried their bodies in an unmarked spot by the side of the road and planted a cottonwood tree on it."

"Why a cottonwood tree?" Remy asked.

"Because they are robust and can grow six feet per year. Lance Conley knew that give it a year or two, it's guaranteed the bodies will never be found as the tree grows big."

Seth stared at his glass. "That was the primary reason my father behaved erratically towards the end of his life. He was guilt-ridden. And the secondary reason, was my father didn't realize Richard had hidden the last two words of his crypto recovery phrase elsewhere —in a keychain under the floorboard of his room."

“Correct.”

“So all this time, the hotel was haunted by three ghosts? Richard and the Solomons?” Remy wanted clarity.

“Not exactly. The kitchen haunting has always been Richard. For some reason, he was so upset over missing the Christmas Eve Feast that his obsession was enough to make his spirit wake up at Christmas time three years in a row. I honestly think he would’ve kept it up forever if we didn’t interfere.” Kari answered.

“The Solomons didn’t do any haunting until recently. When Carson’s car crashed into the cottonwood tree, it woke them up. They saw Velvet and I and were drawn to her because she reminded them of their own cat.”

Carson raised an eyebrow at Velvet, who lay curled up on a plush pillow by Destiny's feet. "And they wanted company — that explains the strange phenomena at Destiny’s house with the cat toys and Velvet's treats.”

"And so it all came together," Remy mused aloud. "Richard wanting his feast, your father's secrecy surrounding his death… and then the Solomons' untimely passing creating additional unrest."

Seth ran a hand through his hair. "All this time we've been living with their stories intertwining with ours." He looked around at everyone gathered. "And it took all of you to untangle it."

He raised his glass. "On my father's behalf, please accept my deepest apologies and sincerest gratitude."

Crystal tinkled in resonant harmony as five flutes touched and echoed. “Here here!” Carson winked sideways at Destiny, pride and affection welling inside him.

Talk soon turned towards lighter topics - preparations for the evening's Christmas feast, the free offerings made possible by Richard's mysterious crypto windfall. As despondency dispersed on laughter and banter around the table, Carson felt a deeper shift permeating his being. Amongst this group of friends, he was feeling the holiday joys in the depths of his bones.

Chapter Nineteen

The frosty twilight wrapped Christmas Hills in a shawl of shimmering silver as Destiny and Carson walked, their breaths mingling with the chilled air. She hesitated, biting her lip before the words tumbled out in a rush.

"So, my mom... she's invited us to dinner. It's nothing fancy, just—well, you know, mom's cooking." A faint blush colored Destiny's cheeks, her hands fidgeting with the fringe of her scarf. "I'd understand if you'd rather not."

Carson glanced at her, his eyes alight with amusement and warmth. "Are you kidding? I'd love to. Besides," he said with a grin that crooked to one side, "After all the elaborate feasts and whatnot, I've been dying to have some real home-cooked food."

Relief bloomed across Destiny's face like the first flowers of spring. She laughed softly, the sound dancing on the wind. "Okay, great. Just... be prepared for the full Diane Mellowes experience." Her voice held a playful note of warning.

Carson chuckled, rubbing his hands together in anticipation. "The more authentic, the better."

"Fair warning," Destiny said with a half-smile as they approached her parents' warmly lit house, the scent of roasting herbs greeting them from afar. "My mom might be a little... intense."

"Intense is good," Carson replied with an easy confidence that seemed to stride ahead of him. "I grew up in a house where silence was the main course at dinner."

DIANE MELLOWES, a loud whirlwind of maternal enthusiasm, welcomed Destiny and Carson into the cozy embrace of her home.

Destiny's gaze fell upon the main course, a golden gratin that seemed to beam up at her with pride. She recognized the dish immediately—the lima bean and sweet pepper gratin from her debut cooking show episode. Her mother had recreated it with gusto, and no small measure of creative license.

"Mom, is that...?" Destiny began, eyebrows arched in surprise.

Diane beamed, nodding vigorously. "Your very own recipe, darling! Well, I added a few tweaks—extra cheese, a pinch more garlic, and a special secret ingredient. It's what makes it a Diane Mellowes' original."

A blush crept up Destiny's cheeks as Carson looked on with a grin that threatened to split his face in two. He leaned in close and whispered loud enough for only Destiny to hear, "Looks like your culinary magic's catching on."

Roger Mellowes burst into the room at that moment, his booming voice cutting through the laughter like a ship through calm waters. "Ah, there's the little chef herself!" he bellowed, clapping Carson on the back loudly. "And our esteemed cameraman!"

Destiny groaned inwardly but managed to maintain a smile as her father continued unabashedly. "Say, Carson," Roger said, "you wouldn't happen to know a thing or two about rebranding and marketing, would you? Our little gift shop could use a new flair."

Carson's eyebrows shot up, but he recovered quickly. "I'd be honored to help out," he said with genuine enthusiasm. "It sounds like just the project I've been looking for."

Destiny watched as her father lit up like the Christmas tree in town square. She couldn't help but smile at Carson's willingness to dive into her world headfirst—and maybe stick around for longer than she'd dared hope.

THE END

If you loved ***Revenge is a Dish Best Served with Eggnog***, then you will love ***The Seer-ious Business of Murder: A Faye Constantine Cozy Mystery Book One***

Available on Amazon

READ an excerpt on the very next page!

The Seer-ious Business of Murder

A FAYE CONSTANTINE COZY MYSTERY BOOK I

The past few weeks had been a whirlwind for Faye. She had been struggling with writer's block on her PhD thesis in neuroscience when she received a phone call that changed everything. Her aunt's lawyer was on the line, informing her that her Aunt Azalea had passed away. Faye's heart sank as she listened to the somber voice explaining that she had inherited something unexpected—a metaphysical bookstore in Paradise Cove, a small town on the northern Californian coast.

Faye was taken aback. She had not been particularly close to Azalea, but she remembered the occasional family gatherings where her aunt would passionately discuss her love for books and the mystical arts. Faye had no idea her aunt owned a bookstore, let alone a metaphysical one, and certainly had never imagined she would inherit such a place.

Leaving her cozy apartment in the college town, Faye embarked on a journey up the scenic coast. Her Fiat, with a teardrop trailer hitched to the back, carried her belongings and mixed emotions. As she drove, Faye could not help but feel a sense of trepidation and excitement intertwining within her.

Glancing at herself in the rear-view mirror, Faye observed her reflection. Her wavy auburn hair cascaded down her shoulders, framing a face that bore the weight of recent stress and uncertainty. She noticed a faint scowl etched on her features. She took a deep breath and let the stress melt away.

Lighten up, Faye! She thought to herself. *All of this just crash-landed in my lap like some pie from the sky. I need to get there, have a cup of hot tea, and relax.*

The tires screeched as the car came to a halt in front of the Mystic Eye Bookstore. Faye's grip on the steering wheel tightened as she took in the sight before her. Nestled in a picturesque, small northern Californian coastal town, the metaphysical bookstore exuded an air of enchantment. Dreamcatchers hung from the eaves, swaying gently in the breeze, while colorful wind chimes filled the air with their soothing melody.

Aunt Azalea owned the entire building, including a small apartment above the bookstore, which would now become Faye's new home. Usually, her aunt had reserved this room for visitors and had not lived in it herself. Faye wondered why Azalea had chosen this arrangement, but decided to explore the answers later.

Faye's heart raced, a mix of excitement and apprehension coursing through her veins. She exited the car, stretching her cramped legs and taking in the salty sea air. As she did so, a woman with her hair up in an elegant bun walked briskly over from the neighboring bakery with a warm smile.

"Hello! You must be Faye. I'm Mabel, the baker from next door. I knew your aunt, Azalea. She was a kind woman and always had time for a chat. I'm sorry for your loss," Mabel greeted Faye with a warm smile, her eyes glimmering with empathy.

Faye extended her hand and shook Mabel's. "Thank you, Mabel," she replied, her voice filled with gratitude. "It's nice to meet you."

Mabel studied Faye's features for a moment, her eyes lingering on Faye's wavy auburn hair. "You know, Faye, you have a striking resemblance to Azalea. The red hair definitely runs in the family," Mabel remarked, a touch of nostalgia in her voice. "She would often come over to the bakery, browsing through books while savoring one of my freshly baked apple pies. Those were the days."

Faye's curiosity was piqued. "I never knew I had a family resemblance to Aunt Azalea," she said, a hint of wonder in her voice. "I wish I had the chance to know her better. Maybe running this bookstore will bring me closer to understanding who she was."

Mabel nodded, a knowing smile on her lips. "Life works in mysterious ways, dear. You never know what secrets lie within these walls and how they might connect you to your aunt's legacy. Knock on my bakery's door if you need anything. And welcome to our little coastal town."

"Thank you, Mabel," Faye replied, returning her smile. "I appreciate your kindness. It's nice to meet you."

Mabel's eyes twinkled as she handed Faye a box filled with various pastries. "Here's a little housewarming gift. Welcome to the neighborhood!"

Faye's mouth watered as she took in the sight of the delectable treats. The succulent and oversized cinnamon rolls beckoned to her, still warm and oozing with gooey sweetness. The giant chocolate chip cookies, their golden exteriors studded with generous chunks of chocolate, tempted her taste buds. And among them, Faye could not help but notice the exceptionally vivid macarons, their vibrant hues hinting at unique flavors waiting to be discovered.

Faye's stomach rumbled, reminding her she had not eaten much during the journey. The tantalizing aroma of freshly baked goods filled the air, mingling with the sea breeze. Her hunger grew stronger, her stomach growled, and her resolve weakened.

"Thank you so much! I haven't had a proper meal in a while. The past few weeks have been... chaotic, to say the least."

Unable to resist any longer, Faye reached into the box and grabbed a cinnamon roll. She savored the moment as she took her first bite, the soft, doughy texture melting in her mouth, accompanied by the comforting warmth of cinnamon and sugar. It was pure bliss.

As she continued indulging in the pastries, savoring each heavenly bite, Faye could not help but appreciate the warmth and hospitality of her new neighbor Mabel.

Mabel patted Faye's arm gently. "Take your time, dear. This town has a way of making things better. You'll see." With that, Mabel returned to her bakery, leaving Faye on the sidewalk.

With no further reason to put off the inevitable, Faye took a deep breath and reached for the door.

As she entered, the faint scent of incense wafted through the air, intertwining notes of frankincense, dragon's blood and palo santo. Amid the subtle smoky undertones, Faye thought she also detected the faintest trace of rose essential oil. Aunt

Azalea's favorite. The melange of scents was both comforting and heart-wrenching.

Faye placed the box of pastries on the counter and surveyed her surroundings. The bookstore was a treasure trove of unique finds, from crystals and tarot cards to obscure ancient texts. The café in the corner, however, was familiar territory for Faye. She had spent countless hours working in cafés during her college years and knew she could easily manage this part of the business.

Reminded of the promise she made herself of a cup of tea on the drive over, Faye headed to the café corner. As she began rummaging through the shelves in search of tea leaves and a kettle, soft footsteps redirected her attention. Faye turned to find an older gentleman approaching her with a warm smile.

Faye took in the sight of his plump figure, wrapped in a flowing robe that billowed around him. He had a distinctive Californian, hippy charm, and the fact that he dressed like a jovial wizard added an element of playfulness to his character.

But it was not just his appearance that drew Faye's attention; it was also his endearing mannerisms and unique way of speaking. The man had a melodic accent that danced on his words, as if he had collected accents from every corner of the world and fused them into his delightful linguistic symphony.

"Ah, you must be Azalea's niece," he said, his voice deep and gravelly. "I'm Bartholomew, the manager of the Mystic Eye Bookstore. You came at the right time. I was just about to close up for the day."

Faye extended her hand, smiling politely. "Nice to meet you, Bartholomew. I'm Faye."

He shook her hand firmly, a twinkle in his eyes. "Please, my dear, call me Barry. Or perhaps Bart would suit me better. Bartholomew sounds far too serious for the likes of me."

"Okay, then Bart it is," Faye could not help but chuckle at his playful suggestion.

"I've been running this place for years. Your aunt was a dear friend. I'll help you with anything you need," He said generously.

"Thank you," Faye replied, feeling a sense of relief. "I appreciate that. I'm sure I have a lot to learn."

With a slight grin, he beckoned Faye to follow him toward the opposite corner of the café. The wall was lined with black and white portrait photos of interesting characters, an androgynous woman with long white hair covered in tattoos, a couple kissing at what looked like a glassblowing studio, and a woman with a curly mane sitting on and painting a giant canvas, another woman sitting next to her, smiling. It piqued her curiosity.

"Bartholomew, what's the story behind these amazing photos, if you don't mind me asking?"

"Yes, of course. These are all local artists in Paradise Cove. We used to have a café manager who was involved in the art scene herself. She took these. Spirituality and arts are branches of the same tree. I think it's only fitting, wouldn't you agree? Now I won't answer any more questions if you keep calling me Bartholomew." He winked.

Faye noticed he would often pause mid-sentence as if to build suspense, making rhythmic cadences that accentuated his speech.

They passed the café's gallery wall and came to a locked cabinet. Through the glass cabinet doors, Faye could see the shelves inside were filled with beautifully crafted tins and glass bottles, each containing exotic teas and elixirs.

"These, my dear, are the treasures of the top shelf," Bartholomew whispered, his voice theatrical. "Teas and elixirs that can transport you to distant lands, heal the soul, and even grant you a touch of magic."

Faye's eyes widened with anticipation as Bartholomew retrieved a small key from his pocket. He inserted it into the lock and turned it with a flourish, revealing the hidden contents within. The cabinet revealed an assortment of exotic tins and jars adorned with intricate labels and vibrant colors.

Bartholomew carefully selected a tin labeled “Sea of Tranquility" and handed it to Faye. "This blend," he said with a twinkle in his eye, "is the key to finding serenity amid chaos. Would you like me to brew you a cup?”

Faye marveled at the delicate aroma that emanated from the tin, a harmonious blend of rooibos, lemongrass, lavender, and something she couldn’t pinpoint.

"I could use a relaxing cup of tea,” Faye remarked.

“Tranquility in a cup, coming right up,” Bartholomew said as he turned the kettle on and continued, “If I recall correctly, Azalea sourced this one when she went to Antiqua. For her, teas were not just for drinking. They were companions on her journeys and a source of her inspiration.”

Faye nodded, her curiosity piqued by Bart's words. She could not wait to delve into Azalea’s world of exquisite teas and books.

"While we're waiting for the water to boil, why don't I give you a hand with your bags? I presume you will stay in the apartment above the bookstore?"

"Yes, I'd love that, thanks!"

They stepped outside, and just as Faye was about to reach her vehicle, a sudden gust of wind swept through the air, and a massive shape tumbled through the air at great speed toward her.

Recipe

JAIME'S HOMEMADE EGGNOG

Serves 8 - 10 (4 cups)

6 large eggs, separate the yolks from the whites

1/2 cup granulated sugar

1 cup heavy whipping cream

2 cups milk

1/2 teaspoon ground nutmeg

Pinch of salt

1/4 teaspoon vanilla extract

Ground cinnamon, for topping

Alcohol, ¼ cup brandy, bourbon, rum or whisky. Optional, see note

Instructions

1. In a medium bowl, whisk the egg yolks and sugar together until a light and creamy texture forms.

2. In a saucepan over medium-high heat, combine the cream, milk, nutmeg and salt. Stir often. Turn down the heat when the mixture reaches a simmer.

3. Start adding the hot milk to the egg mixture, a big spoonful at a time, whisking vigorously. Repeat one spoonful at a time to temper the egg yolk mixture.

4. Once most of the hot milk has been added to the eggs, pour the mixture back into the saucepan on the stove and turn the heat back up to medium-high.

5. Continue to whisk vigorously for a few minutes, until the mixture is just slightly thickened (or until it reaches about 160 degrees F on a thermometer). It will thicken more as it cools.

6. Remove from heat and stir in the vanilla and the optional alcohol.

7. Pour the eggnog mixture through a fine mesh strainer into a container and cover. Plastic wrap and cheesecloth work best.

8. Refrigerate until chilled. It will thicken as it cools. If you want a thinner, completely smooth consistency, you can add the chilled mixture to a blender and add 1 to 2 tablespoons of milk at a time. Blend until the desired smoothness and consistency has been reached.

9. Serve with a sprinkle of cinnamon or nutmeg and fresh whipped cream. Serve in glass mugs or tumblers.

10. Jaime's homemade eggnog can be stored in the refrigerator for up to one week.

Note

While brandy is the most traditional alcohol to pair with eggnog, according to traditional recipes, you can also use a mixture of dark rum and Cognac. If you like your eggnog with more of a kick you can also add bourbon or scotch. But for the most authentic flavor profile, Jaime recommends sticking to brandy, rum, or cognac.

Bonus Recipe

LIMA BEAN AND SWEET PEPPER GRATIN FROM DESTINY

Yields 8 Servings

Ingredients

2 tablespoons unsalted butter

1 shallot, minced

3 cups baby lima beans, can be frozen or canned

1 cup chicken stock

1 bay leaf

Salt

1 tablespoon extra-virgin olive oil

1 large sweet onion, cut into 1-inch pieces

1/4 pound applewood smoked bacon, thick cut, cut into 1/2-inch pieces

4 garlic cloves, minced

2 red peppers, cut into 1-inch pieces, see note

1 tablespoon parsley, chopped

1 teaspoon thyme, chopped

1 cup Parmigiano Reggiano cheese, freshly grated

Freshly ground black pepper

1/2 cup basil leaves, shredded

1 cup bread crumbs

Directions

1. In a medium saucepan over medium heat, cook the minced shallot in 1 tablespoon of the butter. Once softened, add the lima beans, chicken stock, bay leaf, 1 cup of water, and a large pinch of salt and bring to a boil. Cover and simmer over low heat until the beans are tender. Usually 30 minutes. Drain, but save 1 cup of the cooking liquid.

2. Preheat the oven to 375°F. In a large, deep skillet, cook the red bell peppers, onion, and bacon in olive oil over medium-high heat until the onion is lightly caramelized, about 10 minutes. Stir in the lima beans then add in the minced garlic, chopped parsley, and thyme. Continue to simmer for 5 minutes then remove the skillet from the heat. Stir in the reserved 1 cup of cooking liquid and half of the cheese and season with salt and pepper.

3. In a separate bowl, mix the remaining cheese, bread crumbs, 1 tablespoon of butter, and shredded basil leaves.

3. Butter a 9-inch by 13-inch baking dish then transfer the lima beans to the prepared dish. Sprinkle on the basil, cheese, and breadcrumb mix. Bake in the oven for 25 minutes, preferably on an upper rack, until golden brown. Take the gratin out

and let it set at room temperature for 10 minutes before serving.

Note

Substitute the red peppers with fire-roasted red peppers for a sweeter taste. You can also use a mixture of fresh red peppers and caramelized red peppers.

Ada Rayne is an author of paranormal cozy mystery books. She loves to explore the mysterious hidden realms in order to create captivating narratives that resonate with her readers.

When Ada isn't writing, she's traveling with her partner. From wandering through deserted castles, uncovering secrets of ancient ruins, to seeking out ancient alchemical texts and paintings in obscure book shops, often attracting an entourage of creatures from purring cats to shimmering dragonflies on such outings. Stay connected with Ada's paranormal tales and exploits, she loves to hear from her readers.

amazon.com/stores/Ada-Rayne/author/B0CD2PSYYL
goodreads.com/AuthorAdaRayne
bookbub.com/authors/ada-rayne
facebook.com/AuthorAdaRayne
instagram.com/authoradarayne

Made in United States
Orlando, FL
04 January 2024